Bob Moats

I0567374

BLACK WIDOW MURDERS

Black Widow Murders

ISBN - 978-0-9960845-8-1

For information and address:
Magic 1 Productions
P.O. Box 524, Fraser MI 48026-0524
Website: http://murdernovels.com
Cover by Bob Moats

Bob Moats

Other Jim Richards series books by Bob Moats

For a preview or to purchase a book, go to
http://murdernovels.com

What people are saying about the Murder novels by Bob Moats

"I went online this morning and read your book. I thought at first that I would only read a few pages, but got sucked into it and read all 11 chapters. You are a very good writer! I read quite a bit and often pick up "Airport" paperback mysteries to read on a plane. Most of them are dreadful, with obvious plots. Classmate Murders is a much better story than most."
Ray Zink, Entrepreneur, Minn.

"I got up to chapter ten of the Classmate Murders and decided then to buy the next two books." ... "Just finished your third book, the Dominatrix Murders. I thought it was the best one of the three, didn't want to put it down till I finished it. I looked forward to see how Penny would greet (Jim) every day after her show. Keep the books coming can't wait for the next one."
A. Norris, former Naval Corpsman

"If you like mysteries and action then don't miss reading this book..."
Jan Schneider, avid mystery/crime reader

"I finished the book last night, and really enjoyed it. I can only read a book that fast when it keeps my interest, so that should tell you a lot. I would recommend this book to others. I look forward to reading the next installment of the book."

M. K., retired Chrysler Management

"I haven't finished the book yet, when I enjoy a book, I take my time, but I want to buy the other two books. I compare your writing to a Mickey Spillane novel, and I like your style, very narrative. I'm amazed you don't have a publisher yet."

Michael Rasah, Professor of History

"Thanks for making me immortal, love the stories, your friend, Buck."

The real "Buck", George Carver

"Bob, I LOVED it. It reminds me a lot of Colombo, I can see Jim as a regular guy, not a smooth talker, but able to outwit the bad guys. The characters were great and I love the way you describe so many of them. Some of your other characters were fun to read about. I can't think of any corrective criticism. I will have my husband read it, he reads all the time. I think he will love the book too."

Joyce Van Houzen-Stacy, B.A.,M.B.A.

Bob, my brother, Bill, sent all seven of your Jim Richard's novels for me to read. I loved them. They were interesting and fast moving. You did good and I hope you write some more of them. I gave the books to my daughter and now she says she is hooked! I enjoy your books and I want to see more of them. It is hard to find books of this type. Concise and

interesting. We need more books like these. Getting published is a real war. I hope you have good luck with them. You have a talent for writing novels the way I think they should be written. Regards,"
Fred Scharmann, Avon, OH

Murder novels aren't my usual fare but this sweet, suspenseful and often humorous series draws you in and keeps you guessing to the end. I've read all eight (some of them twice) and hope to see more coming soon. I recommend following Jim Richards adventures but take care, murder seems to follow him!
Tia L Brink, Binghamton, New York

Extra special thanks to:

Thank you to all the people who purchased this book. I hope you enjoy it as much as I enjoyed writing it for my faithful readers.

The Jim Richards Family of Readers is listed in the back of the book.

Black Widow Murders

by Bob Moats

Chapter 1

Harvey Trent was prone on his bed in the totally dark room when he felt them crawling on his chest. He had problems before with bed bugs and had sprayed the mattress with some god-awful smelling spray that forced him to sleep on the couch for a week. The crawling continued and he was determined to ignore the damn bugs. Harvey told himself he was probably dreaming and to snub the minuscule creatures, they would go away, but they didn't. Then he suddenly felt something like a large feather brush over his chest, causing the tiny creatures to act agitated and then it happened, the first bite. Then a couple more, then a lot of tiny bites. Now he was feeling pain and a burning sensation, so he got up and went to the bathroom. He flipped on the light and turned to the mirror above the sink, what he saw almost made his heart stop. A dozen or so spiders were hanging on to his chest and stomach still biting.

Black Widow Murders

He screamed and ran to the shower, turned on the spray and jumped in brushing the damn beasts off off his body. He watched as a few went down the drain and managed to get most of them off of him in the stream of water. He batted at the ones still hanging on and finally flicked the last one off. He now was looking at the tiny welts that were forming from the bites and they were burning worse now.

He climbed out of the tub and did a quick drying with a towel, moving back to the mirror to see the red bumps were not going away. He knew he was in trouble as he looked closely to one of the spiders that had landed in his sink; it had a red lantern shape on its back, a Black Widow! He was feeling nauseous now and was becoming dizzy. The phone he thought, he needed help, so he staggered to the living room bouncing off the walls and fell at the table where the phone sat. He managed to push 911 and when the voice came on, he screamed, "I'm dying from spider bites, help!"

As he lay on the floor dying, a dark clothed figure stepped around him, closing the container that minutes before held the dozen tiny spiders. The figure put the container and a plume feather in a back pack and then took out a self-inking rubber stamp from the backpack and pressed it to Harvey's forehead, leaving an ink mark, then the person quickly left the house. Harvey never felt the ink stamp, he was dead.

It was now five in the morning and Joseph Lang, the Clark County-Las Vegas medical examiner, was trying to finish his sandwich just outside the house when Detective Lynn Carter along with her partner, both as a cop and at home, Deacon DeAngelo came up. "Hey Joey, whatcha got?" Lynn asked.

"Ham on rye with horseradish," he replied nonchalantly.

Lynn looked at him for a moment, "No, I mean what have you got for the crime scene?"

"Oh, guy died from spider bites," he mumbled as he chewed his food.

"Okay, why was homicide called in?"

"That's the fun part; he was murdered with spiders, Black Widows. Someone dumped a bunch of the buggers on him and they did their thing and bit him to death." He swallowed the last bite of the sandwich. "Now I can go back in." He crumpled the sandwich wrapper and put it in the pocket of his coat then walked to the entrance of the house.

Lynn stood there not moving and Deacon asked her, "Aren't you going in? I know you really hate spiders but I'm sure they have the crime scene secured."

She looked at him with a fear in her eyes that

he had never seen before, even when confronting a gun toting madman. "One spider is bad; a bunch of spiders is not good. You go in and check it out; I'll wait here for you."

Deacon looked around the ground and said, "There's probably more spiders in this yard than there are in the house right now."

"You are a mean son-of-a-bitch." She said and forced herself to go forward into the house. She saw the body of the late Harvey Trent by the overturned coffee table, the phone still in his hand. He was totally naked and she bent down to see the red welts on his upper body. Joe Lang was checking the body. "I thought a Black Widow's bite wouldn't kill you right away." Lynn said.

Lang looked to her, "Well, one bite would take a short while to kill, but so far I counted fourteen bites, you do the math."

Lynn straightened up on hearing the number of bites, looking around for all those spiders. Lang could sense her tension and said, "All the spiders are gone, either washed down the drain in the tub or smashed by Trent here as he attempted to brush them off. Just my expert opinion."

That didn't help Lynn's tension. Deacon came up behind her and said her name causing her to jump. "Do you want to see the bedroom?" he asked.

"Yeah, sure, we can do that." They walked down the hall and Deacon could see that Lynn was looking all around, checking for attacks from spiders. He was trying not to make light of it, knowing she really hated spiders.

They did a quick exam of the bedroom and didn't see much. "Has CSI been though this room?" she asked.

"Yep, about an hour ago," said Lang from the hallway as he was heading to the bathroom just off the bedroom. Lynn followed him in and they stood examining the sink to see the dead spider in the bowl. Lynn turned and went out after seeing the tiny creature, fearing it would come back to life and jump her.

Lang turned to Deacon still standing in the bathroom, "She doesn't like spiders does she?"

"Nope, I'm the one who has to kill the things if they get in our apartment. I hate them too, but not fear them like she does."

Lynn called to the ME while she was still looking around the living room, "So why do you assume he was killed by someone. Couldn't there have been a nest of them and they decided to attack?"

Lang was coming down the hallway again as she asked this. "I might have thought that too, but

I decided he was murdered when I found this." He went to the body and turned the man's head so it faced upwards and Lynn could see the mark. She got closer and could see it was a Black Widow stamped on his forehead. Lang looked to her and said, "I'd say we have a killer."

~~*~~

Later in the morning, Penny was smiling at camera three as the stage manager signaled to her that her guest was ready. "Vegas, we have a treat this morning, that really funny entertainer, straight from his afternoon show at the Golden Nugget, comedy magician Magic Bob is going to be here live in a few moments." She went on about her guests for tomorrow, she was now having more celebrities willing to sign up for her show and she was thrilled. I was enjoying her happiness; it was good for me also. A happy Penny is a sexy Penny.

She finished the show and went to her dressing room finding me sitting in the make-up chair telling her staff about the crimes I solved in my brief career. She pushed at the chair causing me to stand, I kissed her and she sat to get her make-up removed. "Are you here to annoy or take me to a fabulous lunch at the Bistro?" she asked.

"I was thinking more along the lines of Sonic's." I gave her a smile and she stuck her tongue out at me. Her groupies worked on turning her into an ordinary everyday citizen of Las Vegas, removing her TV show face, but she still glowed in her street makeup.

The girls finished her make-up and I joked, "Can't you make her look like Sheena Easton?" She whacked my stomach and said to blow it out my ear. She stood and I went to pick up Willy from the couch where he was sleeping soundly. He looked dazed and licked my hand; I put him in his doggy purse and slung it over my shoulder. Penny hugged the girls and told them she was really glad they moved to Vegas to continue to do her make-up. Celeste said she was honored to be there and loved Vegas.

We left and went out into the blazing heat and quickly into the car. I flipped on the air conditioning and drove out of the parking lot. It was now just starting spring in the valley, but it was not like back in Michigan where the seasons were recognizable. It was now almost one hundred degrees out in the relentless sun. I wasn't complaining, I spent most of my time in air conditioned rooms. I did take Penny to Bistros for lunch and she was happy.

Then we went to my office to find Lacey looking flustered. "I'm trying to get things organized and Buck keeps moving things on me." I said I'd talk to him and told her to organize the way she wants. I asked how her fingers were doing after the surgeries she had to fix the tendons cut by the criminal Merkins a couple months back after he kidnapped Lacey, Penny and me during the Sin City case. She held up her bandaged hand and said it was better but still hard to move the fingers.

I went to talk with Buck and said, "Lacey is trying to run the front office, she's inexperienced at it so she has to learn, now leave her alone to set it up so she'll know where everything is."

Buck smiled, "I know, I was just messing with her."

"Well, quit it, she's young and I don't want her trying to commit suicide again." Referring to how we met her after she tried to kill herself because of a crime lord trying to set her up for murder. We solved the case but she was still fragile.

"Yeah, I guess I have a strange sense of humor. I'll be easier on her now." He smiled. "So any good cases coming up?"

"Nothing yet, I have more ads going out to the public but it will be a waiting process."

I heard the entrance door open since I installed a little bell on it and went out to see Lynn and Deacon in the lobby. Lynn looked to me and said, "Do you like spiders?"

Chapter 2

Sometimes I couldn't figure Lynn out, as a detective she was hard and determined, but she was fragile in many respects. I never knew when she was being a cop or being a human. Not that cops aren't humans.

"Okay, I give, should I like spiders?" I asked.

"Well, do you?" she asked back.

"I have nothing against them, except those really tiny ones that usually bite when you annoy them. I had a pet tarantula back when I was in my twenties." I replied. I could see her shiver when I mentioned the tarantula, I had a feeling she didn't like spiders. "So, you don't like spiders I take it?"

"No, I hate them, worse than serial killers. Why did you have a tarantula? Weren't you afraid of being bitten?"

"Lynn, tarantulas do bite if really annoyed but the bite is not fatal to the majority of humans. I used to hold the thing in my hand and let him crawl on my arm."

She really had a fit on that, "You are one sick person. How could you even touch the thing?" I could see she was having the heebie jeebie shivers as her whole body was shaking now from an involuntary reaction to the thought of spiders. Deacon was standing behind her laughing quietly. She turned to him and said, "Stop that or you'll sleep with the spiders."

"So what brought this all up, did you find a spider in your unmarked car?" I asked.

She gave me a stare that said to shut up, so I did. "We had a new case this morning; a man was killed by the bites of a dozen or so Black Widow spiders. Lang, the ME says it was murder, they were dumped on him. Then the killer left an ink stamp of a Black Widow on his forehead."

I could hear both Penny and Lacey express their disgust. "So do you think this is a random kill or do we have a psycho serial Spiderman killer?"

Lynn gave me that look again, "I don't know, we'll see. I'm hoping this is an isolated case, I don't want to have to interrogate spiders around Vegas."

That broke the tension, even Lynn had to laugh. Changing the subject, Lynn said, "So how's business?"

"Well, ever since we stopped Merkins, the crime lord of Vegas, and Penny made a big deal of it on her new talk show; we've had a small number of people wanting their spouses followed. No murder cases yet, but I've got a couple billboards going up that have Buck and me looking tough and ready to deal with the underworld."

Lynn's cell phone rang and she answered, listened and hung up. "Crime just doesn't stop, more gangbangers shooting each other. Hopefully they will all kill themselves off and make our lives easier." She signaled to Deacon and they left.

Penny came to the counter now and looked to me, "You actually had a tarantula?"

"Yep, a Mexican Red-Legged Tarantula, and I had a little plastic cage for her so I could take her with me."

"Her, you knew it was a her?"

"Well, I named her Tilly the Tarantula, so she ended up being a she, I have no idea what its sex actually was."

Penny looked to Willy sitting on the desk next to Lacey, "Could Tilly have carried off Willy if you had her today?"

"Penny dear, she wasn't that big."

Buck, who was standing by hallway listening to us said, "We could get one of those big terrariums and a couple of tarantulas for the office."

"I don't think that's a good idea, Buck." Penny

said firmly.

I turned to Buck and said, "Don't even think about buying rubber spiders to leave around the office." He smiled and winked, then went back to his office.

"Lacey, are you feeling better now that everyone from the Sin City case is dead?" I asked.

"Well, my nightmares have gone away and I'm not sleep walking anymore, or at least Mac says I'm not." She blushed when she said that.

"Lacey, it's no secret that you and Mac are living together, after all you are engaged." Penny added.

"And Buck told us when Mac changed his address in his personnel file. Penny and I lived together for almost a year before we married, so it's no big deal."

"It just seems strange to be living with someone; I've lived alone for so long. Mac was the only man I ever had a thing for so it's easy to have to live with him," she said wistfully.

"Okay Lacey, watch Willy for us, I have to go to the billboard company to approve the thing and I need to take Penny along to complain about how bad I look being twenty feet tall."

Lacey and Penny both laughed and I went to tell Buck we were leaving. He was making up a roster for his security guards at the new car lot he had been hired to have his guards watch. He smiled and said, "It's good to be boss."

~~*~~

Lynn and Deacon followed the two cops just about dragging a gang member into the holding cells. He was cursing and screaming about how he'll kill every cop he could. Captain Weber came out of his office and motioned to Lynn and Deacon to come to his office. He told Lynn to close the door.

"I heard about your spider case this morning and when a patrol cop told me the vic's name I did some checking. I thought I recognized the name, Harvey Trent. He's in, or was in, the WSOP, World Series of Poker, big competition at the Rio Hotel this weekend. Trent was two games away from the big million dollar win. Sound to you like a motive for murder?"

Both Deacon and Lynn had blank looks, but Deacon said, "I watched part of that tournament on TV the other night, I remember that guy now. He took the lead from a couple Hollywood stars that were losing big. This puts a new spin on the killing. But why go to all the trouble to kill him with spiders and then leave a mark to show us it was murder?"

Black Widow Murders

Weber waved his hand and said, "That's what you two are going to find out, I'm getting a little pressure from the commissioner to solve this. We don't need murder to ruin the fine reputation of our world class poker tournaments. Besides there is a lot of money at stake here, people attending and betting on the outcome of the games, it's good for everyone concerned. Now do something about this quickly, the next round of games is in three days." He sat at his desk and started shuffling papers; Lynn knew that was their cue to leave.

Outside Webber's office Deacon said, "Three days doesn't leave us much time."

"Maybe we could bring Spiderboy in on this to help." Lynn mumbled to herself.

"Spiderboy, who's that?"

"Tarantula man, you know Jim, he loves spiders, so he can cover for me... us when it comes to the logistics of the case."

Deacon smiled and said, "You'll do anything to get out of investigating spiders won't you?"

"Damn straight, let's go see if we can intrigue him into taking up the cause."

~~*~~

Bob Moats

I was looking up at the amazingly huge picture of me standing with my arms crossed back to back with Buck doing the same. We looked tough. Penny was laughing, not helping my mood. "Do you have to make fun of my projects?" I asked.

"Well, I always said you were a big man in town. Life size even." She had tears coming now from laughing. I happened to like the thing, it looked... well, tough, and I told her so.

"Jim, you are supposed to be smart and clever to solve crimes, not the terminator."

"Well, it says that we will do the job, we are ready for action."

"Watching spouses from outside a house, snooping in back alleys to take pictures of business theft. Hardly a tough man job."

"Yes, but we will be getting more dangerous cases once the word is out. This city has an underbelly of crime that we will take down."

"The only underbelly I see is your gut sticking out from under your arms."

I studied the picture by going back a good ways and she was right, the picture did make me look a bit paunchy. I asked the production manager if they could run it through their image processing software and make me a little less beer belly. He smiled and said he would. I approved the billboard with changes and took Penny out to the car. We drove over to the office again and pulled in to see Lynn and Deacon standing in front of the building. I parked and we went to them.

"What's up troops?" I asked.

Lynn spoke, "We came over to see if we could interest you in a position as civilian advisor to the Black Widow case."

"You really don't want to get near spiders do you?" I joked.

"Now you sound like Deacon. We got here and were waiting for you to get back; Lacey said you went to look at a billboard."

"Yep, me and Buck standing twenty feet tall. So what do you want from me on this case."

"Well, you may have another case, one waiting in your office. We came in and this woman was there talking to Buck in the lobby, we stood listening but we didn't identify ourselves as police detectives on the Harvey Trent case."

"So what the problem?"

"She's Harvey Trent's wife and she wants to hire you to find Harvey's killer because she knows that the police will suspect her, which we will now that we know she exists."

I looked through the front window and I could see her standing with Buck. "Well, let's go kill a few spiders with one interview."

*

Chapter 3

Lynn just stood for a moment, then said, 'We have to take this cautiously, we can't question her properly without taking her in, so we'll just have to let you do your thing and we'll listen for now. Maybe you'll ask the right questions and save us some time."

"Don't worry; I'll handle it like you would. Do you have the rubber hose with you?" I said.

She gave me her stare again, so I just went in. Buck smiled and introduced me to the lady. "Mrs. Trent, you were married to the late Harvey Trent, who was murdered this morning?"

"Yes, how did you know?" she asked.

"I'm a good detective." I said using my favorite line, Penny snorted. I gave her a look and continued, "This is a little awkward, these two

people are Homicide Detective Lieutenant Lynn
Carter and her partner Detective Frank DeAngelo,
they are the primary investigating officers on your
husband's murder. They are also friends of mine
who happen to be here to talk to me about their
case and found you here. Now if you've come in to
hire me to find out who killed your husband, I can
do that. But Detectives Carter and DeAngelo are
going to want to talk to you about your
involvement in the case."

"That's why I'm here, to have you keep me
from being a suspect and prove my innocence." she
said.

Lynn spoke, "I'm sorry Mrs. Trent, but you
already know that we will consider you a suspect
and all we need to do is find out a few facts to
exonerate you. Since you are here, I'll let Jim talk
to you, it may save us a little effort and time. If
that is all right with you if we just observe?"

"Anything to find out who killed my husband."
I could see she was tearing up a bit and Penny got a
tissue from the counter and gave it to her. We had
tissue boxes all over the place, they came in handy.

"So if we could go into my office we can start." I
pointed the way and she went in, followed by Lynn
and Deacon. Penny went around the counter back
to Lacey and sat next to her desk, probably to joke
about my billboard. I went in my office and closed
the door.

Bob Moats

We all were sitting comfortably. Mrs. Trent in my client chair by the desk and Lynn and Deacon sat in two other chairs by the door. I took out a pocket recorder from a drawer and set it on top of the desk. "You don't mind if I record this, it helps keep me straight in my investigations?" she agreed. "Now the police could do their job and solve this for you, why come to me?"

"I want an independent investigation to keep me clear of this. When certain facts come out, I'm going to be murder suspect number one." She glanced to my friends sitting quietly by.

"Okay, start from the beginning, how long have you been married?"

"We married here in Vegas two years ago after one of his poker tournaments that he lost, but he said I was his special win. Lately I was finding that my life was not so glamorous being always second to his gambling. At first I thought he just enjoyed the game, but after these years of following him around the country from poker game to poker game, I realized he was addicted to it. He was good, yes, but not great. He had a flair for being without a tell, hard to read him, which was good in poker. But he was just being himself; he had no feelings, just a desire to win at all cost. I am still married to him, or as I should say now, was married to him, but we were separated, living apart. He was wanting to reconcile but this poker tournament was the big score, a million bucks if he won, and he was getting so close. We have a small apartment here but reside mainly in California, so if he won, I was entitled to half of his winnings in property. So I was all for keeping him alive as you can understand." She looked again to Lynn and Deacon, they gave no response.

"So if he is dead, what do you stand to gain?"

"That's where it gets sticky. He had an overinflated view of himself, he thought he was golden. So he had a life insurance policy on himself, if he died I would get two million dollars, which of course I wouldn't receive if I murdered him. If he was murdered by someone else and I had nothing to do with it, I would gain. So either he dies and I get two mil or lives and I maybe get a half mil. If we were to divorce, I'd get half of what he has now, nothing. Doesn't take much to figure my best advantage or a motive."

"Was there anyone else who may have wanted him dead?" I asked.

"Yeah, six other people in the tournament, both male and female. They had a million reasons for him to be dead." she replied.

"Mrs. Trent, where were you this morning from about..." I looked to Lynn she finished, "Between midnight and four A.M."

"Please call me Stacy, I was in bed."

"Well Stacy, anyone to verify that." I asked.

She sat quietly and then said, "I do have a special friend, who stays with me on lonely nights. He was with me this morning."

"Of course, we'll need his name so we can verify this. My question is, if you had an alibi, I still don't understand why you came to me?"

"The alibi is the problem. He's one of the other competitors in the tournament, so he would be suspect also." She sat back and went silent. I handed her a pad and pencil and asked her to write out any names and contacts I may need to check on this case, she took about a minute to write a few names and phone numbers and handed the pad back. I handed her my rate card and said, "If you still want me to investigate, these are my fees." She said money is no problem and hoped I could help her.

Lynn was smiling and said to her, "Mrs. Trent, we will need you to come in to make a formal statement on this matter. I've heard enough for now but we need to have the name of the man you were with to verify your whereabouts this morning. We are just starting to investigate and will need some more information. Can you come in on your own or shall we drive you?"

Black Widow Murders

"I have my car; I will come in peacefully and cooperatively." Lynn stood, followed by Deacon. Mrs. Trent stood as I did and Lynn told her where to go and she would meet her there shortly.

She went out saying she would be there. I turned off the recorder and looked to Lynn. "This is totally weird; I'm still not sure why she wants me to investigate this. It's all police matters as far as I can see."

"I don't like her, about as much as I like a Black Widow Spider. She's up to something." Lynn said.

"You still want me as an advisor?"

"I think I will, I need someone to wrangle the spiders if we get another murder, I hope not."

I laughed and said, "Just give me a call. When you are done with the Black Widow, let me know and how your questioning went."

Lynn said she would and then went out followed by Deacon. They went to their car after saying good-bye to Penny and Lacey and drove off.

"So what have you two been up to?" I asked cautiously as I came around to the desk.

"This came in the fax while you were grilling the spider lady." She held up a copy of the changed billboard for me to inspect. I had a nice washboard abs look to me now, I liked it, Penny just laughed. "You will be insufferable now every time we see this on the road."

"I've got one going up by the county buildings and one by the freeway and Tropicana, just down the road from here. I can admire myself every morning on the way to work."

"Yes and your head will be about as big as your billboard self." She made a face and taped the picture on the wall.

Buck came out of his office and said, "It's a good likeness wouldn't you say."

I smiled to him and said, "We do look tough don't we?"

~~*~~

The dark figure went into the small room off the basement; it was more of a cellar. The man had on an outfit that looked like a diving suit, rubber and form fitting. He wore a mesh hat with screen like those that bee keepers wore, but this was not an outfit for bee keeping, it was for keeping the Black Widow spiders from biting the man as he gathered the tiny creatures that he raised in the room. He took good care of his babies, catching insects and letting them loose in the room to feed his flock. He couldn't count the numbers of the arachnids that lived there, the count would change frequently as the creatures would battle amongst themselves and when the egg sacs hatched half of the little ones would eat the other half to survive. It was a room in constant change and battle. The man admired the tiny creatures, devoted himself to them. Now he had to gather a few to go out in the world to fight the good cause, extermination of evil men.

The container had a dozen of his babies, and he was ready to go.

**

Chapter 4

I was in my office going through my laptop to find a note I had written with a story idea for my latest book I was starting to write, Mistress Murders, since I had finished the book about my adventures with the Dominatrix case. Penny and Lacey had gone down the street to a sandwich shop to bring lunch back and Buck went out to talk to a new client at the car dealership he had just gotten for his guards to watch. Willy was sitting on my client chair watching me with his head down, trying to stay awake.

Bob Moats

The bell on the entrance door had rang and it couldn't have been the girls, Penny would have called out to me, so I figured it was a client, hopefully. I walked out of my office after putting Willy on the floor, he pranced out behind me. There was a youngish man standing by the counter, who looked to be in his mid-twenties, blondish hair and tan, kind of like a surfer from California. He had on a tank top showing off fairly well developed muscles and shorts that bagged down around his knees.

"Hi, can I help you?" I asked.

"Yeah, you're the P.I. dude right?"

"Yep, I'm the P.I. dude fer shure." I mugged.

He looked at me with a strange expression, then the light bulb went on in his head, "Oh, hey, ya fer shure. I get it now, funny. I need help, you available?"

"I may be, what does it involve?"

"I think I may be in danger, I think someone wants to kill me."

I wondered if he was serious and said, "Okay, let's talk. Come into my office." He followed me in and then saw Willy.

Black Widow Murders

"Wow, a miniature dog. Does he guard the place?"

"He's an ankle biter, be careful you don't make any fast movements." I joked but I think he believed me as he slowly went to my client chair, stepping carefully. I was trying not to laugh; this guy must have indulged in a bit too much medicinal weed.

"What's your name?" I asked.

"Oh, yeah, I'm Freddie Norris, pleasure to meet you." He said holding his hand out, I shook it. "I saw your little detective and security business sign on a taxi at my hotel and came looking for you. I figured you might help me."

"Okay Freddie, why do you think you're going to be murdered?" I asked.

He pulled a business size card from his pocket and handed it to me. I took it and was surprised to see a black widow spider stamped on it.

"That was slid under my hotel room door. I heard about Harvey dying from spider bites this morning, the news didn't say how or why he was bitten, but this card made me think. With Harvey out of the competition, it was better odds for one of us to win. So I thought maybe he was murdered and this card worried me."

"You're going to have to back up a bit. I'm presuming you are in the poker tourney and knew Harvey?"

"Yeah man, I'm in the contention to be one of the winners now that Harvey is gone; he was an awesome poker player, no expressions to give him away. Super primo card player. Now I'm not liking this spider card thing, it's creepy that I get it so soon after Harvey bit the dust, oh, pardon the pun." He gave out one of those goofy giggles you hear in the movies from a stoner. "The news said he was bit by a spider and died, but with this card I think there was more to it."

"I'm not at liberty to discuss the police's case on Harvey's death but I will be happy to look into this for you." I handed him my rate card, figuring I better get this out of the way to see if he had any money. He looked at it and then reached in his front pocket of his shorts and pulled out a wad of cash. He peeled off a couple of hundreds and put them in front of me.

"Man, I'm so close to winning the million, a few dollars is worth it to keep me alive till this thing is over."

"I'm thinking you need protection and I may be able to help you with that." I had seen Buck walk by coming from the back door and excused myself. I went to Buck's office and he gave me his big grin and said howdy. I told him about the man in my office and asked if Mac was doing anything, I wanted to hire him for protection. Buck said he'd call him and have him come in; he only lived a short distance away. I thanked him and went back to my office.

Freddie was now reaching down and scratching Willy behind the ears, he looked up and smiled, "This is one cute dog you got here."

"I like him and he keeps my wife happy." I said that just as I sat and then heard the front door open and Penny yelled that it was her and Lacey. She breezed into my office and saw Freddie sitting and stopped saying, "I'm sorry, I didn't know you had company."

She put a bag on my desk by me, my sandwich I presumed. I introduced Freddie to Penny and he got this look on his face and said, "I know you, you're on TV aren't you?" she said she was and he said he watched her this morning on TV in his hotel room. He was excited over meeting her and I let him ask her questions about her show as we waited for Mac to come in.

About ten minutes later Mac came in and stopped to give Lacey a kiss before he came to see me. Penny was just going out to eat her food and said hi to Mac as he came to my door. Mac is a big guy and nearly fills the door frame as he enters, the kind of guy you want protecting you. He looked a little like a cross between a mob enforcer and a bouncer at one of the swank clubs in Vegas, big and tough. Tough, my kind of image for the firm, I smiled.

I stood, "Mac, this is Freddie Norris, I'd like you to protect him for a few days, just until his poker tourney is over. I'll explain the circumstances about the case, it may be dangerous. You do have your weapon?" He pulled back the opened shirt he wore over his t-shirt to reveal his .38 tucked into his belt. Buck made sure his men were all licensed to carry for various functions he wanted them to guard.

"Good, Freddie this isn't going to be a problem for you to have Mac or a back-up around all the time?"

"Hell no, as I said I want to get through the tourney to win. Not to die here in this desert."

"Okay, I'm going to keep this card; I'll have to show it to the police to let them know that this may be a problem." I turned to Mac, "Take him in the conference room and work out a schedule for watching him and talk to Buck about a back-up for you when you need a break." Mac said he would and they went out. I sat and pulled out my cell phone, calling Lynn. I knew this would just brighten her day to know that the spider killings were only beginning. She came on, I told her it was me and said, "It's not over."

Black Widow Murders

I spent a few minutes explaining the situation, hearing her groan every so often and then she said they'd be over in a while, she had finished with Mrs. Trent and she wasn't convinced of her innocence. But with this new information it may be deeper than we thought. I said I'd be in the office till about five and would see her shortly. I put the card in one of the small plastic envelopes I keep in my desk, in case forensics could pull prints off of it, but I doubted it.

Mac and Freddie were ready to go out and I told Mac to call me if any little thing happened, he said he would. They left and I went to Buck's office and asked if he had worked out his deal with the new car lot and he said it was a piece of cake. "No more problems with Retcho guards?" I asked.

"Nope, they're staying away from us now. I'm not going to fall into his traps again. My men are armed and dangerous now."

That worried me a little but I figured it was Buck's job to keep them in line. We talked until my phone rang and I went to get it. I answered and I heard a voice on the line saying that I had better stay out of it or there would be problems. I asked what 'it' was and the voice said, "just stay out of it," and hung up. This was getting annoying, threats on the phone now.

I went to the SD card recording device I had installed on the phone to record my calls and played back the voice. I listened to it a couple of times then I pulled the SD card from the recorder and put in a new one. I put the card in an envelope to give to Lynn; I had an idea what 'it' was. The Black Widow Spider killer did not like my involvement, but how could he know so soon? Freddie was just here and couldn't have told anyone or could he have? I'd have to ask. I called Mac and asked if I could speak to Freddie, he came on and I said I had to know if he talked to anyone about the spider card or coming to see me.

"Yeah man, I told a bunch of people in my group about it and that I was going to see you. I wanted people to know I was being threatened, safety in numbers, ya know."

"Okay, sit down and write out every name of every person who may have heard you talk about it, everyone, it's important and give the list to Mac, I'll send someone to get it." He agreed and I hung up after telling Mac what was going on.

Penny came to the door and asked how it was going. I looked to her and said, "We got spiders crawling out of the woodwork now."

* *

Chapter 5

Freddie Norris was enjoying the comforts of the Rio Hotel luxury suite as Mac was resting on an easy chair looking out to the Vegas strip from the tenth story window. Mac was also looking at the list of names Freddie had written of people he had told about his situation with the spider card and seeking me out to investigate. I sent Lacey over to pick up the list, I figured she knew her way around Vegas and she'd be happy to see Mac, since he was going to be away for a few days protecting Freddie from spiders.

Freddie was sitting at a poker table he had the hotel bring up for him. There were three other younger men playing cards with Freddie and Mac had insisted he check the men for ID and weapons. They didn't like it but Freddie reminded them of Harvey Trent and they were pacified.

Lacey knocked at the door and Mac had warned Freddie that he was the only person to answer the door. He peeked through the hole and could see the top of Lacey's head standing there, he open the door and let her in. Seeing the cute young girl gave rise to all kinds of excitement from the geeky card players but Mac shot them a warning look, they shut up and went back to their cards.

"Hey baby, I got the list here that Jim wanted. You got any time to visit?" Mac asked.

"I said I'd be right back, I think Jim has his police friends coming to look at the card and he needs the list. But I could come back later after work if you aren't too busy." She gave him a quick kiss and took the list from his hand.

"I'll call you to let you know, I'm still not sure how dangerous this is going to be if the killer does decide to hit Freddie."

Lacey looked worried, "I don't want you hurt."

"Hey, I survived two tours of Iraq; I think a luxury hotel is a little safer. I'll talk to you later." He kissed her and she went off. The geeks at the table were still snickering and Mac walked by saying, "Eat your hearts out."

A half hour later Lacey arrived back at the office, list in hand. Lynn and Deacon had just gotten there and I was showing the card and filling them in on the phone call. I had played the recording for them and said, "I tried the callback number but it came up nothing, may have been a disposable phone. But I do get the feeling that the killer may not like people nosing in on his killing."

"He'd have to know that the police would stick their noses in it, so why worry about you doing that?" Deacon asked.

Black Widow Murders

"Probably because he knew of my superior detecting abilities and was worried I'd expose him." I smiled.

"Dream on Sherlock, he's exerting his authority over the crime, sort of beating his chest that he is the clever criminal." Lynn added. "He probably could care less about you, no offense, but he likes the thrill of getting close to the people hunting him. His call made it a challenge to you. This may just turn into a serial case."

Penny said, "Why not, Jim loves serial killers." I smiled at her and blew her a kiss. "I do this all for you, my love." I smiled. She replied, "Don't go out of your way for me, sweetie."

I took the list from Lacey and she went back to the reception area to work on her filing and sorting of the security guard's personnel files. Willy came bouncing over to her and she put him on the desk by her and rummaged through folders. Buck had left her alone now, he liked having fun with people, but Lacey was too young and innocent to mess with.

Lynn was looking the list of names, all people staying in the Rio Hotel and most of them involved in the poker tourney. "Play the voice recording again," she asked. I did.

I spoke, "Well, it definitely was a man's voice so

we can rule out women, unless they're working with the killer, but I think he works alone. This was a fantasy killing, using spiders instead of just shooting or stabbing the victim. A little more dramatic and weird."

"Weird for sure. Why did he have to use spiders? Black Widow spiders at that." Lynn asked.

"Maybe he was frightened by Toby McGuire in Spiderman." Deacon laughed.

Lynn shot him a look; she was doing that a lot lately. This case was going to stress her out until it was solved. "So what shall we do about the list?" I asked.

"Let's go listen to a few voices and see if any fit." We all stood and went to the lobby. Penny said she was getting tired and wanted to go home, I asked Buck if he could run her home for me, he said he would. I had driven Penny to her station for her show this morning, otherwise she would drive herself, but I wanted to take her to lunch so I drove. I kissed her and said I'd be home in a while.

I followed Lynn and Deacon in my Crown Vic over to the Rio Hotel and into the parking structure. We went into the hotel and I had to call Mac to find out what room they were in. He told me where they were, so we went to the elevators and up to the tenth floor, finding the room. Lynn knocked on the door and it was opened by Mac

41

smiling at us. Freddie was still with his companions playing cards and he stood as we came in. I went to introduce Freddie to Lynn and Deacon and Lynn said, "May I ask you a few questions?"

"Sure, let's go sit over there," he said and pointed to the area that served as a living room in the huge suite. We went to the plush couches and sat; Freddie's friends watched us but were far enough away to not hear us.

"Freddie, how long have you been involved in playing poker?" Lynn asked.

"I've been at it ever since my uncle taught me to play when I was twelve. He said I had a natural ability for the game, he said I was good. So I kept at it and entered a number of competitions around the country, I played online a lot and then came to Vegas for the big World Series Of Poker, the WSOP tournament that they would hold at either Caesar's Palace, the Rio or Harrahs. I had built up a good amount of cash and had enough to enter. I'm finally in the running for the grand prize. Finally after all these years, the cards held good for me."

"Did you know Harvey Trent?"

"Sure we all knew each other, we were a crew, friends and still rivals when it came to Texas Hold-em. I was shocked when I heard about Harvey, then that card came and it wigged me out, man, I didn't like being threatened. I saw that little billboard on the taxi out front for Richards Investigations and Security and figured they'd have someone who could watch me to keep me safe, so went there. I'm not about to die this close to the win." He sat back and smiled.

"Where were you early this morning from about midnight till four A.M.?" Lynn asked.

"I was here with my peeps, playing cards of course, these fine gentlemen right here as a matter of fact." He said pointing to the geeks still hunched over the table watching us. When Freddie brought the attention to them they pretended they were intent on playing cards.

"Are they on your list of peeps you told about the card and going to Richards Investigations?"

"Yeah, they were here when the card was slid under the door."

"What time was that?"

"Oh hell, it had to have been around five A.M. give or take." he replied.

Lynn looked to Deacon, then to me, "Just after Harvey got it. He's moving fast." She turned back to Freddie, "I need to talk to your peeps, call them over."

Freddie called the others and they sauntered

over, looking like a gangsta clan, hoodie tops and backward ball caps, all hip-hop and cool acting for lily white boys. I bet they'd crumble if I came at them with my Glock.

Lynn held her badge out and told them to sit. "Freddie says you pulled an all nighter here playing cards?" They quietly acknowledged her with head bops and grunts. "He mentioned that he was going to see someone about that spider card he got, any of you remember that?" Again with the head nods. "Any of you make any phone calls about the card or his visit after he left?" Now they swayed their heads side to side. "So, if I check the phone records of this room, there would be no calls going out?" Again the sways. "Now I can get a warrant for your personal cell phones to see if there were any calls made, how about that?"

Two of the boys did the head sway, but one just sat still. I saw this and so did Lynn. "What's your name, sport?" she said to the boy in the hoodie. He sat looking blank, not saying anything. Lynn turned to Mac and asked, "Mac, would you escort everyone but this fine young man out of the room for a moment while we talk?" Mac came over and motioned to the group to vacate the room and they did, slowly, watching back to their friend.

The boy sat, now looking a bit worried. Lynn leaned over to Deacon and asked him to sit next to the boy to help him remember any calls he may have made. Deacon sat next to the now frightened

44

boy, sitting about a head taller that the kid. I was trying not to laugh.

"Now you want to tell us something?" Lynn growled. I wasn't sure, but think the boy peed his pants.

**

Chapter 6

"What's your name, sport?" Lynn said.

He was quiet for a minute before Deacon cleared his throat, then he sat up and said, "Johnston, Harry Johnston."

"Well, Harry Johnston, talk to me, you made a call about Freddie going out to see a private eye?"

The boy nodded his head after looking up to Deacon, "Yeah, I did."

"Who did you talk to Harry?"

"I don't know who he was; I just had a phone number to call him if anything goes down with the guys."

Black Widow Murders

"How did you come across this person?"

"He was hanging behind the table where we were playing Hold-em yesterday. I took a break, well, I was eliminated actually and went to the can, he followed. I thought at first he was some pervert but he introduced himself as a reporter and wanted some good dirt on the players. He told me he'd give me $100 to call him anytime something happens with us, any little detail that we do. He said there would be more money later if I did good. I needed the cash so I said I would. He gave me a card with a number on it and left. I didn't care who he was, he just offered me money, so I took it."

"Could you describe him?"

"Wouldn't do much good, he had on sun-glasses and a full beard that covered most his face. I think it was fake. He had no scars or marks that I could see and he had on a hat, like they wear in the Bahamas, you know hemp with a wide brim. His clothes were plain, nothing to make him stand out. I really don't think his description would help."

"Where's the card he gave you?"

"I threw it away, I have a good memory for numbers, it helps with counting cards, but I didn't say that. I didn't need it, so tossed it."

"Did you give him any information about Harvey Trent yesterday?"

"No, Harvey was in a different part of the auditorium, I didn't see him at all yesterday."

"Okay Harry, you're going to do us a favor so we can catch us a killer, I'm going to have our electronic techs put a trace on your phone and we'll have you call him. Maybe we can track him down, unless you know anything more about him?"

"Nope, just what I told you."

"I'll need your cell phone number to get this started," Lynn said and Harry gave her the number and handed her his cell phone. She called the forensics department and asked for someone in electronics. She explained what she wanted and gave them the phone number and they said they'd see if they could do it. Lynn waited and then the person came back and said they had gotten the tower links to his phone and to try calling a number. Lynn looked to me and said she was calling my number and dialed it on Harry's phone. My phone rang and I answered, the tech told Lynn to hold on and then came back saying the cell tower triangulation pointed the call to a cell in the Rio Hotel. Lynn smiled and said to hold on.

"Harry, I want you to call the number and tell your friend that Freddie got a bodyguard to watch him, but didn't like the guy so he fired him and is now alone, think you can do that?"

Black Widow Murders

Harry nodded his head and took the phone back and dialed the number. He put the call on speaker phone and a few seconds later the person answered. Harry identified himself and told the person on the other end of the phone what Lynn told him to say. The person asked a few more questions and Harry made up a few things he thought sounded good, Lynn was nodding her head approvingly. The person said that Harry did good and would be in touch with some more money and hung up.

Lynn went back to her phone and asked if they got anything. The tech said that it looked like the call was received in the Rio hotel again; he asked if we had made the same call as before, Lynn said it wasn't. The tech said then the person was also in the Rio.

Lynn hung up quickly and called for back-up of just her detectives, no sense getting the Hotel upset by SWAT rummaging through the building. She told Warren where to meet and then hung up. She looked to Harry and said, "You, my friend are going to lead us to find this guy, understand!" She stood and Deacon helped Harry up by his collar. I followed them out the door and told Mac to take the guys back in the room and be on guard, the killer may be near. He said he would and I ran after Lynn and Deacon pulling Harry along.

We got to the ground floor and waited at the entrance for Warren and his men to arrive. Harry was looking around nervously, probably hoping the killer didn't see him with the cops. About ten minutes later they showed up and Lynn explained her plan that they would walk around the WSOP auditorium to see if they could find him there first.

Lynn led Harry out front into the auditorium where people were still playing Texas Hold-em and they walked around the perimeter. Lynn could feel Harry was shaking as they stalked the floor, he suddenly stiffened as they came around to a group of people cheering on one man at a table who must have won his game. Behind the people stood a man with a beard, sun glasses and a straw hat. Lynn signaled to her men and they spread out around the table.

Deacon came up behind the man and held his weapon up to the man's back as the rest of the detectives moved close to his sides. Deacon whispered in his ear, "It wouldn't be a good idea to do something stupid, you are surrounded by police and we need to take you out of here quietly. Do you understand?"

The man stood frozen but started to nod his head. Two detectives took his arms and brought them behind his back as Deacon handcuffed the man. Lynn asked Harry again if this was the man, he nodded his head vigorously and she told him to hang back but to follow them. The man was led out of the auditorium and taken to a waiting unmarked car out front and put in the back. Lynn told her men she would meet them back at the precinct. They drove off and we went to get our cars, Lynn taking Harry along. I drove over to the precinct and parked, going into the back entrance and found them standing by the interrogation rooms. Lynn waved and signaled me to go in observation. I did.

She and Deacon went into the room as Harry and I sat on the backside of the mirror watching. The man was seated at the table now and looking nonchalant about this all. He had a cool expression from what I could see under the beard that did look fake. Lynn sat across from him and Deacon stood silently by as Lynn leaned forward and spoke.

"You like spiders? Maybe you used a dozen or so to murder a man this morning?" She paused. His smile slowly faded and he took off the sunglasses and put them on the table. He reached up and started to pull at the beard removing it from his face. A few seconds later he had it all off and laying on the table.

"I'm not sure what you are talking about, I killed no one. If you are talking about spiders, I presume it has something to do with Harvey Trent, I heard he died from a spider bite."

"Try a dozen spider bites, all put on him by you." She picked up his wallet laying with his other possessions and said, "So Mr. Harcourt, you know nothing about spiders, Black Widow spiders. I have men at your apartment now checking it to see if your hoard of the creatures are there. Come on Harcourt talk to me. You had a kid keep tabs on a few players and one of them was murdered and another was threatened."

"I'm not who you think I am, I'm not a killer. I'm a reporter for the Las Vegas Exposed magazine. I had the kid feed me info about the players, you know, kinky stuff, illegal activities if any, the good stuff. When that other kid got the spider card and I got a call from Harry about it, I started to put things together. Murder by bite, my next byline. I was hanging around the casino to see if I could pick up on anything else that may tell me more about the killing. That's all I have for you." He sat back.

Lynn just stared at him and stood. "You better be telling me the truth, or I will have Detective DeAngelo here, take you apart for subjecting me to spiders." She walked out of the room; Deacon followed her leaving Harcourt alone with a cop watching him. Lynn took the wallet to her desk and made a call to the LV Exposed magazine after she called information. She asked for the editor after identifying herself and when she came on Lynn asked if they had a Paul Harcourt on staff. The editor laughed and asked if he was arrested again. Lynn said he is in custody and if she could just verify that he worked there. She said he did. Lynn thanked her and hung up.

Lynn looked to Deacon and me and said, "Crap, we got a reporter."

Chapter 7

"This isn't finished Harcourt," Lynn said as she burst through the door to the interrogation room. I went back into observation; Harry was taken back to the Rio Hotel by a patrol officer at Lynn's request.

Harcourt had a smirk on his face, "This is going to be a great piece for my magazine, the killers and the cops who chase them, but get the wrong people."

"You know if we didn't question a few people we wouldn't be able to catch the real criminals, and you are wasting my time to find him. Now shut up and talk." Lynn was looking frustrated. "I meant stop blowing hot air and tell what you know."

"What could I know?"

"Well, after you got the call from Harry about Freddie going to see the P.I. a threat was made to the man. Now you were the only person other than Harry to know this, who did you talk to?"

He was quiet for a moment; he looked to Deacon standing by the door, "I didn't talk to anyone, maybe Harry told someone else. It didn't come from me."

"You may be a reporter, but that doesn't let you off for the kill. You could be raising spiders to murder people, and using your magazine as a cover. As soon as my men are done at your place we'll talk again." She opened the door and called the guard to take Harcourt to his cell until she needed to talk some more.

"What are you holding me for?" he demanded.

"Suspicion of conspiracy to commit murder. Or for further questioning, whichever you like. It's up to you. I believe you are a link to the killer. Your sleaze rag is not my concern, report what you want, the public will decide when it comes out you impeded a murder investigation and aided the killer. I have friends in the legitimate news reporting media. Maybe they'd like my side of the story. Now when you want to tell me about whom you share your information with, we'll talk."

Lynn told the cop to get him out of the room, and then she and Deacon came to my room. "I hate reporters; they do more damage to good people and cops than the criminals do."

~~*~~

Black Widow Murders

It was now around five P.M. when Mac let room service enter with the cart load of food that Freddie had ordered. Mac checked under the covered food to be sure there were no small crawly creatures riding for free. Freddie's friends had left the room to go get some gambling time in before bed time, leaving Freddie and Mac alone.

Freddie invited Mac to join him in the food, since Mac hadn't eaten lunch so they pulled the cart over to the center of the room and pulled two straight backed chairs to the cart and sat. Freddie had taken off his tank top and shoes and just had on his baggie shorts.

Mac lifted the cover over the burgers that smelled tasty and put one on his plate. He reached for the fries that were under another cover as Freddie filled his plate with whatever food was in front of him. Freddie greedily wolfed down the food and reached for the silver plated decanter of what he figured was wine. He removed the top and went to drink from the decanter just as something popped out of the bottle. Mac was watching Freddie and saw the tiny black dot drop to Freddie's face, he jumped up and knocked the bottle from Freddie's hand and was beating his face to smash the spiders that had followed the first one out.

Freddie was screaming bloody murder as Mac knocked the last of the tiny creatures from Freddie. Mac stood and looked to the decanter on the floor to see more of the creatures coming out. He reached into his cargo pants pocket and brought out a small aerosol can he bought on the way to the Hotel earlier. It was a Pyrethrum aerosol that would kill spiders, so he took aim at the decanter and let loose the spray. Watching the spiders curl up and slowly die, he turned to Freddie and checked him for any spiders that he may have missed. There were a few on the table and on the ground by Freddie, so Mac sprayed the area. Freddie had now retreated to the suite's door and was just watching Mac work, his eyes about popping out of his head.

"Fuck man! I could have swallowed the bastards! And the ones I didn't swallow would have been all over my face! Shit!"

Mac quietly checked the area and saw no movement now. He pulled his cell phone and speed dialed me. "I think you need to get over here and bring your friends. We just had a spider infestation."

~~*~~

I told Lynn what had happened and we drove over to the Rio and up to the tenth floor. Mac was at the door now, and we came in to see the scene just as Mac had left it. Lynn had Warren and three other detectives along and told Warren to go down to room service and track the person who brought the cart up. He left with one of the other detectives and Lynn cautiously went to the decanter still on the floor surrounded by dead spiders. Mac explained what had happened and how he had picked up the pesticide spray for protection. I told him he was in for a bonus for his actions and he smiled, "It's all in a day's work."

"How could the killer know that Freddie would drink from the decanter?" Lynn asked.

I looked to the food cart and then pointed, "What do you see here?" I asked.

She studied the cart and suddenly said, "No glasses. The killer left the glasses out. He probably figured Freddie would want the wine and being a kid, just drink from the decanter, like milk from the carton."

"Very good Dick Tracy." I smiled.

Freddie was still shaking, "Why would anyone want to kill me? I didn't do anything to anyone, other than win at cards. Is this a reason for murder now?"

Deacon spoke, "There has to be a connection between Trent and Freddie. Something that someone didn't like."

Lynn walked around the decanter still on the floor and called CSI to come and get the evidence, glad that they would take the dead things out. "Yep, there has to be a connection, so Freddie lets talk about it. Did you know Harvey Trent very well?"

"Just by reputation and we hung a little, just like everyone else. We were poker buddies, everyone spent a lot of time together," he answered.

"Where are you from Freddie?"

"I'm from Santa Barbara, California. I lived there for sixteen of my twenty-four years, started out in Palatka, Florida. My parents moved to California due to my dad's job."

"What did he do?" Lynn asked.

"He was a civil engineer; he decided what roads got paved and how the stop lights were timed. Nothing spectacular, no one had a beef with him."

"I could have disliked him if he set up the stop lights here in Vegas." Deacon said.

"What about your mother?"

"She sold beauty products, but she was a tough woman, no one messed with her."

"Okay, what about you? Do you only play poker or have you another job to fund your addiction?"

Black Widow Murders

"I had a trust fund from my Mom's dad, when I turned twenty-one I was given half the money and when I'm twenty-five I get the other half."

"How much are you talking about?"

"A cool hundred grand already, hundred grand next year."

Lynn looked to Deacon and me, "Not much to kill for."

"How much do you know about Harvey Trent?"

"He was some kind of computer software designer, mostly games for PC's. I talked to him about it one time and he wasn't very open about his work. All top secret, hush-hush stuff. You know corporate espionage stuff. I didn't care, I don't like computer games, the cards are my draw."

Lynn told me she knew most of Harvey's past from talking to his wife, but wanted to see if he shared information with his poker competitors. He did. Lynn turned to Mac, "Do you think you'll be able to stop the killer again? He's not going to be happy that you prevented his kill."

"Let the fucker try something again, I'll be ready." He held his aerosol can like brass knuckles and shook his fist.

I said, "I may have Buck send another man to

help, doesn't hurt to have back-up." Mac said that would work for him. I went off to the side and called Buck to tell him about the incident and send another man.

He said, "I'll call someone and have them there before long and I'm still at your home. Penny asked me to hang in until the pest control people get here. She started looking at the shrubs and bushes around the house and found a number of spider nests; she got a bit freaked, so she called the exterminators."

I had to laugh and Deacon looked to me wondering what was funny. I told Buck I would be there shortly and hung up. I told Deacon and Lynn what Buck had told me and Lynn said, "Smart woman." She looked to Deacon and asked, "Find out if our apartment building sprays for spiders." Deacon winked at me and said he would.

**

Chapter 8

Lynn, Deacon and I stood outside the suite as Warren and the other detective came up, "We searched for the porter who delivered the food cart, but were told he was missing, I wonder why? I asked for his information and was told to go see human resources. They weren't too cooperative, I called the Captain and he got on the horn and had some high mucky-muck in the Rio bosses call to the HR lady and told her to help us or look for another job. She was real cooperative then, here's the porter's address and stats."

Lynn looked at the card Warren handed her and gave it back, "Go track him down and bring him in for questioning, keep him over night. I don't think the killer would be stupid enough to deliver the cart himself, so let's see what is going on. Go get him." Warren left followed by two of the other Detectives, Lynn asked the third one to hang in till the other body guard showed up. Lynn looked to me and said, "Go get lost, I've been at this all day, up at four in the morning to go chase spiders and this has been one long day. I'm done." She looked to Deacon, "I need one of your fantastic massages, baby." He turned red and smiled to me.

"I'm out of here before you two get all crazy and do something you'll regret." I saluted them and went to the elevator. I got to my car and looked around, I don't know why, I just did. I didn't see anything out of the ordinary, so got behind the wheel and drove home. I was coming down the road just before our home, and I could see the exterminator's van in the drive. Since Penny requested the service and it was after business hours, the call was probably considered an emergency, so it would cost more. I'd try to get her to pay for it, but knew deep down it would come out of my checking account.

Bob Moats

I drove around the exterminator's van and Buck's T-Bird and pulled into the garage. I stood watching the man spray the shrubs for a couple minutes, seeing the panic of the spiders in their webs. I felt sorry for them; they were just protecting our yard from insects. I went into the house and through to the back patio door. I figured Penny was probably in the pool, but found Buck, Lacey, Willy and Penny all in the pool. I sat on a chair and watched them swimming around until Penny saw me and swam over to the side of the pool, smiling.

"Hi Sweetie, have a hard day fighting crime?" she said wiping the water from her face. Buck came up and said he sent one more of his guards to the Rio to help Mac, I thanked him.

I looked over and saw Willy coming up the pool steps, Penny laughed and said, "I taught him how to find the steps and get out himself." Willy came flying over to me and I picked him up carefully since he was wet. Penny sitting on my lap wet and slippery was okay, Willy was just wet. I reached over to a chair full of towels and put one on my lap and set Willy on it, he turned around a few times and plopped down. I heard a noise behind me and turned to see the exterminator spraying around the fountain statue and pond. He smiled, came over and handed me his bill, I flinched. He said he would come back in 8 weeks to spray again, then left. I took a quick look to the bill and my heart skipped a beat or two, or three. "It would have been cheaper to hire Mac and his spray can to come over to do the job." I said.

"Yes, but they guarantee that the spiders will be gone for at least 8 weeks. It's good to know that we will be spider free till then." Penny smiled and swam off. Buck said, "Maybe we're in the wrong business."

"Whatever. I'm really not figuring this Black Widow case. Is the murderer just a nut job or is this a calculated killing spree with a motive? So far two poker players have been targeted for murder, could this be a rival card player, or someone tipping the scales for bet wagering? Oh, and give Mac a good bonus for saving Freddie Norris' life. I'd hate to think if Mac hadn't been there, we'd have another death on this case. Mac is good people; he's quick and huge; tough like all our men should be." I laughed.

Buck pulled himself out of the pool; he was wearing his khaki everyday shorts in lieu of swim shorts. He went to the towel on a chair and started to dry. "I could tell Mac was a good man when we first met. He was smart and experienced, I liked him right off."

"Yep, you got lucky with him," I said as I watched Lacey swimming, she had a rubber glove on her bandaged hand. I was glad everything worked out with Lacey and Mac, they were a cute couple. "Are you and Lacey on good terms now?"

"We always were on good terms; she just didn't like me moving her files. I was just messing with her, but I apologized and said I'd leave her alone now." I nodded and said that was good.

"Anyone feel like a late night Bar-B-Q?" I asked, they all liked the idea so I went in to get some pre-formed burgers from the fridge and fired up the incinerator. We all enjoyed the burgers and Penny whipped up a salad to go with it. Then around seven, Buck said he was going to drive Lacey home and then he was going into the office to check his guards before they go off to the car dealerships, then home to Maria before she went to work. I thanked him for his help with the extra guard, he grinned and they went off.

Penny and I sat at the picnic table relaxing when my cell phone rang, it was Lynn. "I'm finished for the night; I hope you don't want something?"

I could hear her laugh and then she said, "No, there's no crimes happening, just wanted to say that we are going to question all five of the people in the group that Harvey and Freddie were in for the WSOP finals, tomorrow morning. If you want to listen in, I'd appreciate it. You do occasionally come up with good ideas and clues."

"Hey, I solve half your cases for you, without me crime would run rampant in the streets of

Black Widow Murders

Vegas," I said with a laugh.

"In your dreams, but you do help a lot. So we're starting the questioning tomorrow at the Rio Hotel, if you want to go visit Mac and Freddie, we'll pick you up from there, say around nine-ish."

"Sounds good to me, I'll see you then." We finished and I disconnected the call. Penny was throwing out the paper plates and cleaning up the picnic table. She turned to me when I put my phone away, "Anything new on the spider case?"

"Nope, Lynn is going to question the other poker players in the morning and asked for my input." I said.

"They actually listen to you?" she smiled.

"I'm the guru of crime solvers now, didn't you get the memo?"

"Must have been lost in the pile of unfounded stories that I threw out today. I've got three Elvis impersonators on the show tomorrow, one is supposed to be in some records book for being the best of the older Elvi."

"Elvi, that sounds like a disease. Don't bring home any blue suede shoes or spangled suits." I paused remembering when we came to Vegas to get married and we almost were hitched by an Elvis minister. Penny hated the idea, she wasn't fond of

Elvis. "Knowing your disdain for Elvis, why are you having three of them on your show?"

"This is Vegas, baby. Elvis has a history here and I have to cater to the masses even if I can't stand him, I just have to grin and bare it," she said and took a running leap into the pool one more time. I just sat at the table with Willy watching her swim.

Morning came early as always for me. Willy was licking my face and I pushed him off. Penny was up and making breakfast for herself, getting ready to go to her studio and smile for the cameras while putting up with the Elvi.

I stumbled in and sat at the snack bar watching her breeze around the kitchen. She plopped down two pieces of toast for me, I thanked her, and she kissed me, and then went off to her car. I shared the toast with Willy and heard my cell phone ringing. I ran to the bedroom where I left it on the bed stand, answering the call coming from Lynn. "Good morning, did you forget to tell me something?"

"Just wanted to give you a heads up, this morning Warren and his men finally found the porter who brought up the food cart to Freddie, he's dead. Seems he was killed by spider bites. Too bad, he must have known who the killer is, the food delivery was set up by Spiderman and he murdered the porter to cover his identity. Too, bad. Are you still coming in this morning?"

"Yeah, I'll be stopping in to visit Mac and I'll meet you there." We finished the call. I looked to Willy and asked him if he was afraid of spiders, he yipped once and wagged his tail.

**

Chapter 9

Shortly after Penny left, Lacey came by to pick up Willy. We had given her the responsibility of taking care of Willy while Penny was working and I had crime things to do in the mornings. "Good morning." I said as I took Willy to the door with his purse. Lacey smiled and said, "It's a beautiful morning."

I handed the dog to her and said, "I'll be in later today, I'll call to keep in touch, and Penny should be in after her show. Have you heard from Mac this morning?"

"He called me to say everything was good at the hotel. He and the other guard took turns watching Freddie, but Freddie didn't sleep very well, so they played cards most the night," she said.

"I hope Mac didn't lose any money."

"No, he didn't have any to lose, they played for peanuts." She laughed and continued, "Mac said he was cleaned out in just a few hands, Freddie is a good poker player." Lacey gathered up Willy and said she'd see me later and went off.

I was dressed and ready to head out after I made an inspection of the shrubs to see if the spiders were gone. They were. I pulled the Crown Vic out of the garage and drove over to the Rio hotel, parked and went up to the tenth floor and knocked on the suite's door. Mac answered.

"Good morning, have you been informed as to what is going down today?" I asked.

"Yep, Lynn called me earlier and asked to have Freddie up and ready to go be questioned." He turned as the other guard was coming out from the bedroom, "Jim, this is Dontae Forte, the other guard." I shook hands with the rather large black man. "Dontae, this is our other boss, Jim Richards."

"Pleasure to meet you, Mr. Richards," he replied.

"Please call me Jim; we're family, not formal." I said.

Freddie came flying out of the bedroom, wearing the same clothes he had on yesterday. Mac leaned to me and said quietly, "At least he showered this morning, or Dontae and I would have thrown him in." I laughed.

"Did they catch the killer yet?" he asked and came to me.

"Freddie, we are working on it, but now we need to talk to all the players in the finals to see if there is a connection between all of you. Oh and the guy who delivered your food last night was found dead by spider bites this morning, so this is not over yet."

Freddie looked stunned by that news and sat on the chair at the poker table. "Damn, what is going on?"

"Murder most foul." Dontae said quietly. I agreed.

~~*~~

Buck was at his desk when Lacey came in the front door and turned Willy loose. Willy ran into see Buck and jumped around until Buck petted him. Lacey was filling his bowl with the dog food we kept at the office and Willy heard that, running out to eat. Lacey went to Buck's door and said good morning just as the entrance door's little bell rang. Lacey went back out and met a very old woman with a cane coming into the lobby.

"Good morning, ma'am, how may we help you?" Lacey offered.

"I need some big, strong men to get rid of some punks," she replied. She looked to be in her seventies, wrinkled face and had almost white hair. She limped which was why she had the cane. Buck had heard the big, strong men part and came out to see what was needed.

"Good morning ma'am, may I help you?" Buck asked.

"Wow, you are a big one. Are you one of the security part of this business?" she asked.

"I'm the man. I take care of security, now what kind of security do you need?" Buck asked.

"I'm Adele Morris, my husband Eli Morris and I own a house near us and we have some unruly tenants, a bunch of drug-addled punks. We served them with an eviction notice but they refuse to leave. I was hoping that you may have some way of getting them out?"

"How long ago did you give them the eviction notice?"

"A week ago, and they still haven't left."

Black Widow Murders

"Why not get the police to evict them?"

"They won't do anything about it, unless there's a crime, they said we had to evict them ourselves. My husband is too old and sickly to do it, so I'm asking for your help."

"Come into my office and we can discuss this." Buck gave her his walrus smile and led her into the office.

"You're not going to get me into your office and seduce me now are you?" she asked.

"No ma'am, I would never take advantage of you." Buck kept smiling.

"Damn." she said quietly but loud enough to make Lacey laugh.

Buck winked at Lacey and said, "I'll even keep the door open."

"Your loss, big boy." she wobbled into his office and went to sit in Buck's client chair.

~~*~~

Lynn and Deacon, followed by Warren and two other detectives arrived at the room around nine and asked if we were ready to start our day.

Freddie asked what they were going to do and Lynn said she had everyone else in the final phase of the competition gathered in a conference room to do some questioning.

"Am I still in danger?" Freddie asked.

"There's always the chance the killer may try to go after you again, but we'll be more prepared now that we know there have been more attempts. With Trent, it was just one killing but the attempt on your life says that the killer is not done. We need to talk to everyone to see what the connection is that the killer is using to murder people. So let's go start the questioning."

She led us all down to a room just off the WSOP convention hall where there were four persons sitting around a table. Two uniformed cops stood watching the people, as Lynn went to the head of the table after telling Freddie to sit.

"I'm Homicide Detective Lieutenant Lynn Carter; these men are Detectives DeAngelo, Warren, Smith and Davis. This other gentleman is Jim Richards, civilian advisor and private investigator. I will be asking you a few questions so we can get to the bottom of Harvey Trent's murder and the attempted murder of Freddie Norris yesterday." The people at the table all started asking questions at once; Lynn held up her hands and asked for quiet. "I'll explain everything in detail just sit and be quiet, I'll get to each of you in a moment. Now I want someone to explain the game procedure to me. How are the finals arrived at?"

Lynn turned to Freddie since she knew him and asked him to explain. Freddie took about ten minutes going over the details of how people were eliminated and narrowed down to the final six people who would have competed in this weekend's competition for the million dollars. Now five with the death of Harvey Trent.

Lynn looked at the list of names she had of the people before her and said, "I'd like to talk to Joe Kepler. Please follow me to a room we have for the interview." She took him to a small room off the side of the conference room as the detectives and I followed.

~~*~~

Buck asked Adele if she would like some coffee, she said no, "but a shot of whiskey would be nice," she said.

"Sorry, I'm a reformed alcoholic and there is no liquor in the office." Buck replied.

"Too bad, it would loosen you up a little." she grinned at him.

Buck was wondering what kind of marriage

she had if she kept hitting on him. "Adele, I need to know more about your situation to help you."

"Well, my husband and I rented our extra house to a young man about two months ago and he started moving people in and they have parties all hours of the night, drugs and drinking, sex and other debauchery. The neighbors started to complain to us and we warned them, but they didn't stop. We finally had it and my husband went and got one of those eviction notices and gave it to them. They laughed it off and we can't get them out."

"Okay, you gave the notice a week ago, are they past the time given to evacuate?"

"Oh, hell yeah, they should have been out yesterday, we told them but they said they were staying."

"All right, I need you and your husband to do something for me then I can do something about getting them out. Give me your address and I'll come by in an hour and we'll start." Buck handed her a pad and pencil and she wrote the address and stood. "How much is this going to cost us?" she asked.

Buck smiled and said, "For you I'll just charge the hourly rate for my men, figure about one hundred dollars and I guarantee our work."

The old lady smiled and opened her purse and took out a billfold and removed two fifties, handing them to Buck and saying, "If there's more of a charge let me know." Buck thanked her and said he had to make arrangements and would be at her home shortly. She thanked him and went out of his office. On her way to the entrance door she looked to Lacey and said, "He tried to get fresh with me, but I held him off." Then she went out. Lacey laughed out loud.

**

Chapter 10

In the small room, Deacon had set up chairs and a small table for the questioning. It reminded me of the interrogation room at Metro only without the mirror. Joe Kepler sat at the table looking confused; Lynn offered him water which he wanted. She poured the water into a paper cup from the pitcher Deacon had brought in for them, and handed it to Kepler.

"Joe, you are in the finals for the big prize, how do you feel about that?" she asked.

He perked up, "Great, I've never been this close to the end before; it's a real great honor." He smiled.

Bob Moats

The door opened and a uniform cop brought Lynn a folder. He said it was the files she requested that were stalled back at Metro, they just arrived. Lynn opened the folder and rummaged through the papers until she found what she was looking for. She pulled out a sheet of paper and set it on top of the folder and read it quickly. "Joe, this is your rap sheet, it tells me everything you have been arrested for or convicted for, and you know what I don't see, anything, you're clean." She smiled to him.

"I wouldn't do anything that would make my mother mad at me." He smiled back.

"Such a good boy. It says that you are thirty-seven years old and from Bloomington, Indiana. How long have you been on the poker circuit?"

"About ten years, I have been doing it professionally for about three years."

"So you have an investment in winning?"

"Well, we all do, a million dollars goes a long way now days."

"How well did you know Harvey Trent?"

"I've known him for about a year, since he came on the circuit. He was a decent guy, real quiet, and kept to himself."

Black Widow Murders

"How would you have rated him in the finals? Think he had a good chance of winning?"

"I'd say either him or Freddie would have gotten to the top easily enough."

"After Freddie, who do you think would have the next best chance?"

"Sara Feinman would have done well."

"What about yourself? Where do you rank?"

"Oh, I never put myself in ranking order, its bad luck. I just play hard and if I win, I win."

"You do want to win, don't you?"

"Of course, stupid to be going all this way and not want to win."

"How badly do you want to win? Enough to murder for?"

He looked stunned, "I would never kill a human, it's against my religion, I'm a devout Christian, Southern Baptist."

"I'm sure your mother wouldn't like it either." Lynn said with a smirk. "Okay, go back out with the others and send in Sara."

Bob Moats

~~*~~

Buck had finished at the Morris' home and with the paper he now had, he and his men walked down the street to the house they had to empty. Buck came up to the door and took the spare key Eli Morris had given him and opened the front door. He positioned three of his men just outside and took one of his men in with him. He stood just inside the front door surveying the situation. There were two men sitting at a table in the small kitchen just off the living room and two other men laying on the couch and a recliner. The men at the table looked stunned as Buck and his man came forward.

"Who the hell are you?" One man asked.

"Well, you were supposed to be out of the house yesterday, and I'm the new tenant as of today." He held up a paper, "This is my lease on the house and you are trespassing, so vacate the building or we will help you leave." Buck growled.

"You and what fucking army?" The man said as he stood, he wasn't tall but fairly well built, and had tattoos up and down his arms.

"Marko," Buck called out. The three men on the porch came in the door. They were part of Buck's guards, the men he had hired from various Harley motorcycle shops around Vegas, so they were all bikers. Buck had them wear their colors to identify what club they rode with. The man standing at the table looked shocked and reached for a gun he had at his back. Buck had the drop on him and shot first, winging the man as Buck's men piled on the other men in the room. The two men on the couch and chair came up and they wrestled with Buck's men but it didn't last long, they had the punks on the ground in quick time. The shooter was on the floor now holding his arm and yelling about his rights. Buck saw the drug paraphernalia, cash and various weapons and pulled his cell phone calling the cops.

About a half hour later, Buck had explained that he was the legal tenant of the house as of today and he was trying to eject squatters, but they gave him resistance and he had to use force to finish the job. He showed the cops the drugs and weapons and then Ted Moran, a cop Buck knew came in and told the first responders that he would vouch for Buck. The punks were escorted out in handcuffs, and before the cops arrived Buck had his men put on the jackets they brought with them that said SECURITY across the backs, hiding their club colors.

Ted smiled at Buck, "If it's not fake Federal agents in your office or being jailed on a false assault charges, its hoods in your home. You lead an interesting life, Buck." Buck grinned and said his men had some cleaning to do. Ted left after getting the report finished up and taking names of Buck's men.

Bob Moats

Adele and Eli Morris toddled in to see the mess that was made of their house. Eli was having a fit so Adele took him out to sit on the porch before he had a coronary. Buck laughed and said for his men to throw everything out to the curb that Adele said wasn't part of the house. The remaining cops were collecting the drug paraphernalia and weapons they found around the small house as Buck's men filled garbage bags with trash that was strewn around the house. Adele was following Buck's men around flirting with them, Buck had warned them about her.

"Adele, my lease on this house runs out tonight at midnight, so you can rent it again to someone else, just check their background carefully. I can do that for you, so let me know."

"Thank you Buck, you took care of it quickly and without too much trouble. Are you sure you wouldn't like a ride with a more mature woman?" She gave him a demure smile.

Buck smiled and said, "I have a live-in girlfriend, she's a showgirl at the Tropicana, she'd murder me if I fooled around with you, but thanks."

"Oh, well. I tried." She said as she went off to talk to the other men.

~~*~~

Black Widow Murders

Lynn had Sara Feinman sitting at the table and asking her basically the same questions.

"How's it feel to be the only woman in the finals?"

"I like it just fine, thank you."

"I assume you really want to win this prize?"

"Of course, I'm showing the men that women can be just as good at Hold-em as they are. This is a time for females to take a stand."

"Enough to kill for?"

"Of course not, I don't play that game; I play for real with the cards. If I can't win legit, I won't play. Killing off the competition doesn't prove your worth; it just shows you can't do it without cheating."

"Do you know anything that you can tell me about Harvey and Freddie that would cause someone to want to murder them?"

"About a million dollars worth of motive, but as I said, I do it legit like."

"So do you have any suspicions about who could want this to happen?"

"Nope, everyone is in the game, we want to win the glory along with the money, but not enough to cheat. Murder is cheating."

"Thank you, please go back and send in Harold Carlisle for me." Lynn asked. Sara stood and left.

"Do you think the killer could be a spider woman?" Deacon asked.

"It's possible, but the percentage of women serial killers is way too low to say she did it, but anything is possible for a million dollars."

Lynn had spent an hour and a half talking to all four of the card players; she had already talked to Freddie but called him in one more time.

"Freddie you barely escaped death, what's your take on it now, have any clues as to who may have wanted to do this?" Lynn asked.

"Oh man, I don't think anyone of the finalists would do this, I've known these people for a while now and they seem all square and good. I'd look to the bettors; the ones putting down tons of money on who they think will win, maybe enough to tip the scales for their favorite to win."

Lynn mulled this over a bit then turned him loose. She stood and looked to me, "Any buzz on this?"

"Nope, I got nothing, sorry. There has to be more to this than cards. Something just doesn't feel right. Are you going to put protection on the other players now?"

"I think we better, it would look bad if we didn't and had another body turn up." She looked to Warren and said, "Put details on each of the players and if they don't like it, too bad. Tell them we'll put their objections on their tombstone."

**

Chapter 11

"No, don't say that, it sounds insensitive, we have to be politically correct now days." Lynn said. "Just be firm and diplomatic, but watch them carefully. The killer almost slipped through us by putting spiders in a drink decanter. Expect anything."

Warren and his men left the room and we went back into to the conference room. Lynn explained to the players that they would have protection until the killer was apprehended, so Detective Warren was going to set up everyone with officers to watch over them. Surprisingly no one objected, I guess it was that or death.

Lynn finished with them and turned it over to Warren as we went back out to the convention hall. I said, "I'm going to the office to check in, if you need me, call."

"I'd like to take a vacation right now, but duty calls, take care and see you later." Lynn said, and then I went out to my car.

I got to where I had parked and saw the note under my windshield wiper. I didn't like notes on my car, it meant that either someone hit my car or a threat on my life was being made. It was a threat. I called Lynn and told her, she and Deacon were just coming out of the hotel and came over to me. I carefully showed her the note.

"I doubt there will be prints on it, but may as well turn it in to forensics." She read the typed note, it just said, "Richards, keep out of this and tell your cop friends they won't stop me." and it was now stamped with a smaller spider than the one used on Trent's forehead.

"Has anyone checked local stationary stores to see who made the stamps?" I asked.

"Yeah, after we found the stamp on Trent's head, I had men going to every store in Vegas but nothing turned up. If it was ordered through the internet, we would have no way of finding the right place. For all we know, the guy is clever enough to make them himself." Lynn said.

"Since this was on your car, which is the only twenty-one year old Crown Vic in Vegas, so not hard to spot, I would think about watching your own people now. The killer knows you." Deacon warned.

"Yeah, I was thinking that too. The note was put on my car while we were in the building and none of the players were out of the rooms at anytime, so that gives them all air tight alibis. We need to widen the search now." I said.

"Yep, it's going to be harder now that we've eliminated the players. I was rooting for Sara to be the killer." Deacon smiled.

"You always hope the women are the bad guys don't you?" Lynn said.

"Well, it breaks up the monotony," Deacon said.

"I'll break you up." Lynn smirked at him.

"Okay kiddies, I'm going to protect my little family. Don't start fighting in the parking lot, go home and take it out there," I said and got in my car.

I arrived at the office after stopping at a nursery store, the gardening kind, not babies. I bought up the last five Pyrethrum aerosol cans that they had, I felt protected now. I drove into the secure parking lot behind my office. I noticed that Buck had a guard in the booth by the gate, I wondered if Larry, our landlord, was paying us for the service. The guard recognized me and waved me through.

I parked and went in the back door and to the lobby. Buck was there with his men and they were celebrating something with snacks, colas and Sprite. Buck saw me and took me to my office where he told me the whole story of his adventure. I said that was great and we went out to have some snacks. Penny was sitting behind the counter and was smiling at me. I went and kissed her, and asked how her day was; she said she had most of the cast from one of the Cirque du Soleil shows. "They were all over the stage and swinging above it, it was fun." I distributed the aerosol cans around the office explaining to everyone what they were and how to use them.

After everyone had settled down I related the day and how we had to be on our toes watching out for anything suspicious arriving here. They all said they would and then Buck's guards all went off to do their own thing. I offered to do lunch for Lacey and Penny, Buck went to his office to take care of business. They said it was a good idea, so I gave them cash and sent them to the sandwich shop again; I liked their ham and Swiss on rye.

I sat at the reception desk as the front door

opened and a delivery man came in with a package. He held out a clipboard and I signed, wondering who would send a package. He left as it struck me; I picked up the package and immediately took it to the back parking lot yelling to Buck to follow me. He came out of his office and out the door behind me.

I set the package out on the lot and stood back calling Lynn, explaining what I had. If it was a bomb, that would be new, but it may be spiders. She said she'd have bomb squad out ASAP and hung up. Buck and I stood waiting, I did go over once to examine the package but saw nothing unusual about it. The return address was from Vegas but no personal or business name.

A few minutes later the bomb squad came driving in and over to the package, they deployed their van and got their equipment out. Lynn and Deacon drove in shortly after; just as the bomb squad was x-raying the box. The x-ray showed no wires or anything large like a bomb, just small dark items crammed into what looked like foam peanuts. One man wearing a heavily armored suit was taking cutters to the box to open it. As he slowly opened the top of the box, the contents suddenly exploded, not from a bomb, but from springs like a jack in the box. Spiders were flying everywhere; the man was screaming and pulling off his suit. The other bomb squad officers grabbed fire extinguishers and were spraying him down. Buck ran back into the building and came out with three of the aerosol cans and handed one to me and one to Deacon. We went around the lot by the box spraying the ground.

Lynn had retreated to the back door of the building just as Penny and Lacey came out. Lynn stopped them and explained what was happening. The three of them went back into the building, far from the spiders. I was not amused; this was intruding on my own turf and my family.

CSI came rolling in and took over the package, collecting the spiders and the contents of the box that propelled the spiders out of the box.

"Clever of the killer," I said to Deacon and Lynn, "If that package had been opened inside, the spiders would have been all over everyone. Whether they would bite or not was not the point, they were a warning. A scary warning." I looked to Penny and Lacey down the hallway and said, "This has just gotten personal, I really want this fucker."

About a half hour later, everything was cleaned up and I went back into the office followed by Buck, Lynn and Deacon. "I think we are spending more time in your office than at Metro, maybe we could set up a police mini-station here." Deacon laughed.

"I'd feel safer if you did," Penny said.

My office phone rang and I went to answer, "Clever of you to take the box out of your office, but that won't stop me from my mission." I was holding my hand over the phone quietly yelling for Lynn, she came in the room. The voice continued, "You can't protect everyone, watch your back." Then he hung up. I went to my recorder and played the call to everyone. Lynn asked for a copy and I made one quickly on the computer and gave her the spare SD card.

"He was watching us; he was nearby and could see us. There are surveillance cameras around the perimeter of the building, maybe we'll get lucky and he'll be on one." I took Lynn and Deacon down to Larry the landlord's office, he was shocked to see all of us pile into the room and asked what we wanted. Deacon knew him well and told him they needed to see the surveillance tapes from the last hour.

Larry took us to a small room in the back where he had a ton of electronic equipment set-up. Lynn looked to him and asked if it was all his. He cleared his throat and said it was. He pointed to the banks of monitors along the wall and said to take our pick. Lynn and Deacon went to them and Larry showed how to run the things back to where we needed. After about fifteen minutes of fooling with the digital recordings, Deacon spotted something on the monitor he was watching, a parked station wagon just outside the fence, and someone inside with binoculars. Larry showed how to zoom in and they got it as close as possible and watched the man. His face was obstructed by a hat he wore and he put the binoculars down and picked up a cell phone.

I said, "That's probably when he called me."

The man then drove off but his plates were not in the frame to be seen. But they had the make and color of the car. Lynn called for an APB on the car, saying to stop every damn car of that make and color in the city. "We may have him yet."

**

Chapter 12

Lynn sent a couple men to track down the delivery company to see where the package came from, but the box had no markings from any particular company so the search would probably be futile.

"What ever happened with Stacey Trent, Harvey's wife?" I asked as we went back to my office. "Is she still my client since yesterday?"

"I don't know about her client connection, but we ruled her out as a murder suspect. She came in for questioning and we talked but she started getting uncooperative, which sent up flags. She decided not to tell us who the card player was that she spent the night with when her husband was murdered. But she did tell us which motel she spent the night at and according to the surveillance tapes, we could see she entered the room at nine and didn't leave till after six the following morning. We never could see the man's face, he was careful to hide his identity. Unless she crawled out the bathroom window, she couldn't have killed him. So if she's still your client it's up to her."

"The last thing she said was that she hired me to find the killer of her husband, so I may still be on the case." I said.

"When we asked if her lover was one of the finalists, she said he was eliminated last week, so he may not be on the list of future victims." Deacon offered.

"So we have no suspects as of now. This case is going well," I said with a smirk.

~~*~~

After he left from watching the circus of police trying to open his box full of spiders, the man drove to Albertson's food store at Maryland and Flamingo Road and left the stolen car there. He walked to the bus stop and got on the north bound bus up Maryland and took a transfer over to his sanctuary up by the Fremont Street area. He entered his building and went immediately down to the basement, checking the door on his little spider ranch, being sure it was still sealed well. He may have cared for his creatures but didn't trust them with his life.

He went over to a corner of the basement to the tables he had set up with his ancient computer and turned on the aging CPU, watching the lights flicker to life. He removed the gloves he wore to prevent fingerprints on the car he took from a nearby parking lot and took off the hat and jacket he had on when he played delivery man for the package. He was lucky to find a delivery person's jacket in the lost and found box he had upstairs, and a hat of the same color set the disguise off nicely. He smiled at the thought of actually delivering the package himself, the fools not knowing it was him.

The old CRT computer monitor lit up and the man sat on the chair staring at the screen waiting for the internet to come up. It finally winked to life and he typed a few things on the keyboard bringing up Twitter on his screen. He smiled as the timeline scrolled down with all the people posting their 140 character sentences talking to everyone and yet no one. He read the posts as they went by looking for one person in particular, a certain woman called by the screen name, @LadyLucky. His love was deep for her, even if she didn't return the feelings. He stared to the wall behind the computer at the printed copy of her avatar, the tiny picture that would show when a person typed a post. He copied it from her profile and enlarged it so he could admire her. It wasn't the best picture, the woman would never let her whole face be seen, just parts, like her eye, or a side view in sunglasses. The man had cut and pasted the parts together and taped them to his wall, an almost grotesque Frankenstein likeness of the woman.

From her profile he learned that she lived in the Las Vegas area; he found her one day while he was ranting on about things that were wrong with the world. He felt he was given the right by his God to speak against the evils of the world. @LadyLucky answered him by questioning his attitude about sin, since she lived in Sin City. He chatted with her for a short while and found her refreshingly attractive. She wouldn't give him any personal information but after a few weeks of chatting with her, he found out a number of things about her.

Lately he found out she had been flirting with a number of men and this disturbed him. Many times he would lurk in the background just watching her talk, and every time she would speak to the men he would fume. He checked the men she was talking to by their profiles and found out she liked men who played cards, either for fun or professionally. He had a disdain for card playing, it was the devil's work, gambling and losing money.

It was then when God spoke to him telling him to vanquish the evil-doers and use his tiny creatures do the job. He now had purpose for his life.

~~*~~

Penny came in around noon, fresh from her show. She had on a few local celebrities extolling their talents and promoting their shows. Penny was enjoying a decent success from her show since she took over from the previous host who left for a weather job in Denver. She was happy and this show had less stress on her than did the show in Detroit, she had built in celebrities here.

"I'm hungry," was all she said to me as she entered my office finding me alone and reading the Review-Journal newspaper.

"So, what am I to do about it?" I asked.

"Feed Me!" she said sounding like the plant creature Audrey II from "Little Shop of Horrors".

"I gave blood at the office," I joked.

"I want juicy meat and onion rings, now." She pulled at my arm and I stood.

Black Widow Murders

"Okay, don't have a cow, man."

"No I'll eat the cow, so get moving."

We went out to the lobby and I told Lacey we were going to Sonic's and asked if she wanted something brought back. She thanked me but said she brown bagged it today.

"Are we paying you enough?" I asked wondering about the brown bag comment.

"Yes, you are paying me just fine, I had some left-over meatloaf since Mac has been working and made a sandwich out of it," she laughed.

Penny started growling about wanting meatloaf, so I turned her to the door and out. We drove over to Pecos and into the drive-in, parking and placing our order.

"So how are the poker killings going?"

"We don't have a clue, unless something falls into our laps soon. So who did you have on your show today?"

"We had a promoter for the WSOP finals this weekend, explaining that people could still get in bets on the remaining players. It gave me chills to think they were betting against the dead player. Is Freddie still alive?"

"Yep, I'm going to talk to him today, a real heart to heart so I can see if he has anything he hasn't told the police. Lynn is getting frustrated with all the dealings since yesterday. I think she wasn't prepared for so much going on, plus the spiders."

Our food arrived by the roller skating waitress and Penny wolfed down her burger and fries in record time.

"I guess you were hungry, you're not pregnant are you?" I asked slyly.

She stared at me then burst out laughing. "Yeah, sure, an almost sixty year old Mom, I don't think so."

"Women have children later in life now days."

"Yeah, well I don't have to worry about that." Penny had problems when she was younger so she never could have children.

"We could adopt, like Brad-gelina, some little starving child from Detroit." I said as I finished the last of my onion rings.

"Do children in Detroit speak English, I don't want one if he or she can't understand me," she smiled.

Black Widow Murders

"I've heard they are teaching English there now. I just wish more people in Vegas would speak English. Sometimes I think I'm in in Mexico."

We finished up and returned the car tray to the waitress and drove out. "Do you want to go to the office and spend the day with Lacey or go with me to interrogate Freddie?"

"I like Lacey, but I'll follow you around for awhile," she replied.

I pulled into the Rio Hotel parking lot and found a spot up close to the entrance. I pulled my cell phone and called Buck. He was in the office now and I asked him to keep an eye out for any strange goings on. "I don't think the spider man will try anything again, but you never know." He said he'd be on alert and I hung up.

We went in and up to the tenth floor; I had called Mac and said we were coming up, so to get Freddie prepared for my arrival. Mac opened the door and Penny and I entered. Freddie was sitting on the couch still in baggie shorts and tank top, no shoes though. Dontae was sitting on a straight back chair watching a basketball game on the television; he turned to say hi to us.

"Hey TV lady, how are you?" Freddie asked. "I watched you this morning; you really had that WSOP promoter going in circles."

I looked to Penny; she said she'd tell me later. I saw Freddie was playing with what looked like a Blackberry phone, he was texting. I asked who he was texting to.

He smiled and said, "Oh, I'm not just texting, I'm on Twitter, talking to a very nice woman, she calls herself Lady Lucky."

**

Chapter 13

"Twitter, eh. I joined Twitter about ten months ago to promote my books. I go by murdernovels, you can follow me if you want, I'll follow back."

Freddie was busy typing with his thumbs, "There, I'm following you. I hope you're not boring. I hate it when people fill my timeline with boring crap."

"So who is Lady Luck?" I asked.

"Lady Lucky, she's a poker groupie. She is always on when the players are tweeting; I think she's even meeting personally with some of the guys. She doesn't come out and say it but its there."

Black Widow Murders

That peaked my interest. "Did she tweet with Harvey?"

"Now that you mention it, yeah, Harvey was bragging one night about this woman he met online and when he said her name the other guys all got a laugh out of it, she was making the rounds with everyone. He was a little offended that she was a groupie."

"Another question, yesterday when you got the spider card, after you told your friends you were coming to visit me, did you tweet that?"

"Yeah, now that you mention it, I did. I tweeted in the cab going to your office. Wow, you don't think that could be a connection?"

"Well, it's something to look at; do you remember who all was online then?"

"Damn, I have over fifteen thousand followers; don't even ask who all were watching my tweets."

"Yeah, sorry, I only have about two thousand followers and they are hard to keep track of. Was Lady Lucky on at that time?"

"Nope she wasn't, last night she said she was busy with some business, but didn't say what."

"Do you know where she lives?"

"Hey, yeah, she lives here in Vegas, now that's convenient. With all the WSOP tourneys going on here, she has a big pool to play in."

I looked to Penny, "This puts a new light on the case. I need to get to a computer and call Lynn."

Penny and I were back in my office and a half hour later Lynn was entering the lobby yelling that she should put a desk in my building. I was in my room at the computer.

"It would save you some time, I imagine. So I went to talk to Freddie and he tells me he is on Twitter and all the poker boys have a follower groupie called Lady Lucky who keeps tabs on everyone. Freddie said he tweeted about his coming to see me, so I figure either this woman is feeding the killer information; she is the killer or there is someone else on Twitter who watches the poker players too and is the killer. I don't know how much trouble it is to get a warrant for her information, but I had a thought, I'm online right now in Twitter, I have an account, so I'll watch her."

"You're on Twitter?" Lynn laughed.

"Hey, it helps with my book promotion. Anyway, I'm on right now, and I'm watching Lady Lucky tweet. I sent a follow message and she accepted it, so she is in my timeline."

"Timeline?" Deacon asked.

Black Widow Murders

"Yeah, it shows what everyone is typing and scrolls off the bottom as new tweets are made at the top. Lady Lucky is quite a flirt. She's hitting on every card player online. I had Freddie make up a list of the guys in his group of players and finalists along with the screen names they go by." I handed the list to Lynn, she showed it to Deacon. "Strange names they pick," Deacon said.

"Yep, to identify themselves, stand out from the crowd, Freddie is AcesHigh and right now he is talking to LadyLucky. I called him and asked if he could engage her in small talk and see if he could set up a meeting with her before the final game. So far she looks interested," I said.

"None of these guys know who this woman is?" Deacon asked.

"So far no, Freddie said those men who may have met with her aren't telling either. Which makes me wonder why. Is there something about her they don't want to admit to? Ha! She is sending Freddie a DM, something is brewing."

"DM, what's that?" Lynn asked.

It stands for a Direct Message, a private message that no one else can see, I hope she is going for the meet. I'll send Freddie a DM and ask him if she did." I did some typing and hit the enter key and waited.

"Yep, she's interested; Freddie is playing it up good. He said she wants to meet at the Wayfarer Motel tonight. Wow, the Wayfarer is where Lacey's murder case occurred. Freddie says he agreed and will meet her at nine o'clock in front. He gave her his information about who to look for, she says to get a room before she gets there."

"Boy, where was the internet when I was younger?" Deacon said, "it's a chick magnet."

Lynn gave him her nasty look, he smiled and shut up. "Don't get any ideas, and I'm going to monitor your computer usage now."

"Hey, I only look at porn, I don't pick up women," he joked.

I reached for my Treo cell phone and dialed Freddie, he came on, "You done good Freddie, we'll be at the hotel about a half hour before you meet her and follow you up. Hopefully this will lead us to the murderer." He said he'd be waiting and hung up. I turned to Lynn and said it's arranged. I looked back to the computer and said, "She's still online, flirting some more, I'm going to watch for a while to see if she says anything else that would tell us about her."

Penny said, "You're just a voyeur, I'm glad you don't sit at home and play on the internet, I'd divorce you."

Black Widow Murders

"Not since you found out how much I'm worth dead." I joked.

Lynn raised an eyebrow and asked, "Is this a cause for murder I should know about?"

"I'll fill you in later." Penny smiled. Penny kissed me and said she was going home to soak in the pool, I said to keep the property alarms on, she said she would and went out the door to her car.

~~*~~

Now the man was pissed, he watched Lady Lucky set-up an assignation with one of the men. When he saw the man's name he was even more incensed, it was the man he tried to murder at the hotel just for talking to her. The same man he had to kill an innocent person for just to hide his identity. But his God would allow him a few discretionary kills, just to get to his goals. Now he had to rid Freddie before he could deflower Lady Lucky.

He sat back in his chair thinking how he could get his playthings into Freddie's room or car if he had one, but he knew Freddie didn't. That damn bodyguard had spoiled his first attempt; maybe he would have to kill both of them. It would have to be another attack in the hotel suite, and soon, Freddie was going to meet with his love in just five hours.

The man looked to the lost and found box he had dragged down from upstairs and had gone through it to find different disguises so he could continue his kills. He had an old janitor's uniform hanging in the basement that he hadn't used in a while and an idea came to him. He went to the uniform and took it down studying it, yes it might work. He placed it on his desk and then put on the rubber protective suit and helmet, then went to the door of the spider room after he picked up the container.

He banged on the door a couple times to frighten away any spiders lurking around the door and opened it carefully watching for any escaping creatures. Satisfied that none had left the room, he entered and flipped on the light. The sight of the mass of webbing and the tiny dots of his pets sent a shiver up his spine. He had respect for the creatures, but was a little afraid of them.

He used the tongs from the wall to gather about a dozen of them in the container and went back out of the room. He set the container down and took off the outfit, hanging it next to the spider room door. He went to get the backpack that he carried his things in and stuffed the uniform in and carefully checking that the container was sealed tight, he placed it in the backpack.

He put on a ball cap and sunglasses and went

up the stairs and out to his own car he had parked in back of the building. He drove to the parking lot of the Rio Hotel and walked around to the back of the hotel to where the employees entered and deliveries were made. It was a little hectic now since there were many deliveries of food and supplies for the WSOP convention, so no one noticed him slip into the building.

He walked around until he found what he was looking for, a maintenance closet. He went in and set his backpack down and put on the uniform he brought. It was pretty generic so he wasn't worried that he would stand out. He placed his backpack inside the maintenance tool cart and put his container on the top of the cart next to the tools. He opened the door and wheeled the cart out and over to the service elevators. He arrived at the tenth floor and found a maid in the halls. He approached her and said, "Hi, I forgot my passcard to get in the room that has a plumbing problem, can you let me in 10-D so I can get done and get out of here."

The maid was Mexican and barely spoke English but he conveyed his story again and she nodded, letting him in the room next to Freddie's. He thanked her and she went off. He had done his research and made a few calls earlier yesterday to find Freddie's room for his prior failed attempt. He looked up to the air duct in the ceiling of the room and took the ladder off the cart and went up to the duct, opening the grillwork. He was thankful for his experience in custodial maintenance when he had worked in various hotels as a younger man. The air duct was big enough for him to crawl in and went over to the next room. He looked down through the grill work and could see Freddie sitting below him at the card table next to Dontae and Mac. He quietly positioned himself so he could drop the spiders on them. He was getting ready to open the container when he noticed Dontae looking up to him.

Dontae squinted his eyes then they went wide and he jumped up pushing Freddie back as he drew his gun and fired at the ceiling. The man let out a yell and dropped the spiders through the grill and crawled back quickly to the other room. The three men were trying to avoid and yet kill the spiders and that gave the man time enough to get back out of the ductwork, down and pushing the cart over to the service elevator. In the elevator he took his backpack out and quickly took off the uniform and shoved it down the elevator shaft. He exited at the main floor with his backpack and disappeared in the crowd of employees and service people.

**

Chapter 14

Dontae had said he saw movement behind the grill of the ductwork but couldn't really see the person's face or whether it was even a man or woman. I said he was in for a bonus also for his actions, which should make Buck real happy.

"The killer is getting desperate. He has tried two kills on Freddie. Now did this have something to do with his meeting of Lady Lucky?" I said as I watched the CSI on the ladder checking the ductwork.

"Well, he had time from the Twitter contact till now to set this up. I'm going with that connection." Lynn said as she stood away from the dead spiders.

"So are we still good to go for the meeting with Lady Lucky?" Freddie asked from the couch as he ate a sandwich he ordered through room service. Mac had searched the porter very carefully, and then checked the sandwich just short of taking a bite to make sure it wasn't poisoned.

"Yes, Mac is going to drive you to the motel, then get into my car leaving you with his car so you can meet with her." I said.

"Am I allowed to have a little sex with her before you arrest her?" Freddie grinned.

"No you're not!" Lynn growled. "We'll take her into custody when she arrives and makes herself known. That's the extent of your place in this."

"Oh, well, hope she's the one you want." He smiled as he swallowed the last bite of sandwich.

One of the CSI techs came in the room showing Lynn the container that had held the spiders. He said, "We found it on the floor of the next room, must have been dropped in the killer's rush to get out." Lynn thanked him and hoped they could get prints off it.

We finished up in the room and got Freddie wired for the meet, to cover all bases. We went down to the lobby and Mac went to get his car and then back to pick up Freddie, as we brought our cars up. We drove up the Boulevard to the Wayfarer Motel where there were a couple of unmarked cars already waiting. Mac parked in front of the building and then got out telling Freddie to get behind the driver's seat. He came to my car and got in, we sat back waiting now. I had my window down and was parked next to Lynn's car so we could talk.

"What are you picking her up on?" I asked.

Black Widow Murders

"Any number of things, suspicion to commit murder, solicitation if she asks for money. I did mention to Freddie to cover that, ask her if this was going to cost him. We'll also bring her in to question her in regards to an ongoing criminal investigation. Hey, I hope she spits on the ground, we'll take her for that too." Deacon smiled as he finished talking.

Just at nine o'clock a car pulled in and parked down from Freddie. I could see him trying to get a look at the driver of the car, when a woman got out. We couldn't see her right away, there was a tree blocking our view from where she parked. She came down the sidewalk in front of the motel and I was trying to figure out where I had seen her before when she came into view.

"Holy Crap, it's Stacy Trent, Harvey's wife." Lynn yelled quietly.

Freddie had his window down and we could hear them on his wire, "Hi, are you Lady Lucky?" His voice came across the speaker from the radio receiver. We could hear her say she was and she went to his car and leaned into his window.

"You got to be AcesHigh? How are you doing and did you get a room?" she asked.

"Yeah, but I need to know one thing, is this going to cost me, I'm sorry to make it sound like you are a hooker, but I need to know?"

She laughed, "Hell, stud, I do this for fun, but I don't object to donations. Say a hundred to the cause would be nice."

Lynn clapped her hands together and said, "We got her for solicitation, that will make things a little easier to handle."

Freddie asked, "Did you know Harvey Trent?"

"Why'd you ask that?" she looked a little shaken.

"Well, he was murdered and I've had a few attempts on my life, just wondered if you knew anything about it?"

"Come on Aces, let's have some fun, don't mess this up."

Lynn was coming up behind her now and said, "Sorry Stacey, but I'm going to mess this up for you. Stacey Trent, you are under arrest for solicitation and suspicion to commit murder." The other detectives were gathering and Deacon put the cuffs on her while explaining her Miranda rights. She glared at Freddie who just stared ahead, not looking to her. She spit at him. Deacon said, "There's that spit I hoped for." He took her to a waiting patrol car that just pulled in from across the street and put her in the back. "Have a nice ride." He said as he closed the door. Mac went to his car and told Freddie to move over. We all left the motel and drove back to the precinct; Mac drove Freddie back to the Rio Hotel to continue his protection.

The uniform cop took Stacey to booking for solicitation and then walked her to interrogation where we waited. Lynn went in to the room and sat across from her.

"I now have a feeling why you wouldn't tell me the man's name you were with on the night your husband was murdered. Weren't you afraid he'd go tell his little buddies that you were Harvey's wife?"

"I never told anyone I was Harvey's wife. Harvey was on Twitter too, I never even told him I was there," she said quietly.

"So explain to me what was going on, why the charade?"

She sat looking around avoiding the question, then she looked to the table and said, "I wasn't happy with my marriage as I told you, I knew Harvey was on Twitter, so I used our other computer and got on also to see what he was up to. After a while I couldn't get off it, the damn thing is addictive. I was suddenly finding men who were attracted to me, and they were poker players. I have this thing for poker players. I set up a couple meetings with one of the men and it was great. No commitments, no names, just pure sex. I started to do it more often, hell, Harvey was always gone off playing cards so I had plenty of time to fool around. He made it easy for me. I would even talk online to Harvey just to tease him; he never knew it was me. I was with one of the men the night Harvey was killed, I couldn't believe it might have been one of the guys on Twitter, but I just couldn't stop talking and setting up meetings. I'm not a hooker, when Aces asked me that I just thought, what the hell, makes it more of a fantasy to ask for money. I do it just for the pure sex." She went quiet.

"Stacey, I don't believe you had anything to do with your husband's murder, but I think there is a connection between the poker playing and the online chatting. Someone is getting the information from the people chatting and we need to know about your habits online, who you may have talked to and their names. If you cooperate I may be able to make the solicitation charges go away. Will you help?"

She spoke softly, "I'll do what I can, if you can help me get help, rehab or something to get this addiction to sex out of my head."

"I'll see what I can do, now write down as many names that you can remember of men you talked to online, if you need to, our computer whiz can get you online and help to list your followers. That sound okay with you?"

Black Widow Murders

She agreed, as Lynn pushed the notepad and pencil to her. Lynn excused herself and came to our side of the glass. "So we have to now dig through the online world to find our killer?"

"I'll keep watching the Twitter streams, I think if you could get her password, I could see her followers better and maybe find someone who has more of an interest in her than just card playing. I can also check her private messages to see if there's something there." I offered.

"I'll put it to her, that's not something she may give us, a warrant might help, but maybe she'll be cooperative." Lynn said with a sigh.

"May I talk to her, she is still my client." I smiled and Lynn gave me a go ahead sign with her hand. I stood and went to the room where she was sitting and still trying to remember names. She sort of smiled as I came in and sat across from her.

"Kind of a hectic day, eh Stacey?" I asked. She just sat quietly writing on the pad. "Are you still my client?"

She looked up and asked, "Have you found my husband's killer yet?"

"I'm working on it, I'm not some TV detective who solves his cases in an hour, it takes time and cooperation from people to track a killer. Can I expect cooperation from you?"

She stared again, "What do you think I know that can help?"

"I need your Twitter password so I can dig around to see who has been keeping tabs on the poker boys. Can you trust me with that info? You can always change your password later. I need more fuel to fan the fire and you can help."

"I give you my password and you snoop around, is that it?" I nodded, she leaned forward, "If it will get me out of this faster and find his killer, I'll give it to you."

I waited then she said, "the password is for gedda bout it."

**

Chapter 15

I said, "Well, if you don't really want to tell me..."

She interrupted, "No, Mr. Big Shot Private Eye, it's..." and she wrote it on the pad of paper, "4geddaboutit".

"Ah, sorry, the phrase threw me. Okay, now is

it all right if I go into your account to snoop around?"

"I got nothing to hide, go ahead and find the killer. It will make me happy and very rich." She leaned back and gave me an evil little grin. I stood, thanked her and went out.

Lynn and Deacon came out of the observation room.

"I still don't like her," Lynn said.

"Yeah, well, I have doubts too, but I need to follow her online stream to see if it has anything to do with this case. Or we may be off on a wild tweet hunt." I said as Lynn stared at me, shook her head and walked away.

"Well, I thought it was funny," I called.

"Not really," Deacon said.

"Well, I thought so."

"No, it wasn't." He followed Lynn as I stood there smiling to myself.

I looked at my watch, it was just now almost ten and I had it for the day. I caught up to Lynn and Deacon and told them I was going home and would see them tomorrow.

Bob Moats

"Don't get addicted to Twitter, and watch out for the wild tweets." Lynn spoke as I was leaving; I showed her my stiff middle finger, yelling, "not funny".

~~*~~

Earlier that evening the preacher looked down on his tiny flock of mostly homeless, hookers and people of low self-esteem who needed the boost that the preacher was able to give them through his sermons and praises. They gathered in the tiny missionary chapel just off Fremont Street in the seedy part of the downtown area, filled with shops selling everything from tobacco to condoms and the cheap motels that charged by the hour. After an hour of preaching and sermons, the preacher paused at his pulpit and studied the faces of the worshipers judging their obedience to him and their God. He stood tall and raised his hand in praise yelling, "Can I hear a hallelujah!" He called to them and they gave their praise back.

"My friends, you have come to me because God has called upon you to follow the path of righteousness and to bring down the unholy work of Satan flowing through the demon cards that the men and women of the WSOP seem to flaunt in the face of the Father. Say hallelujah!" They all praised to the Lord. "We are the chosen ones to go to the heathen temple that is the Rio and raise our voices in worship and praise to cast out the demons who play in sin and degradation. Gambling and fornication! This is Sin City and we need to cast out the sin, make it wholesome again for righteous people to live and breathe the God given air of our beautiful desert city." He looked around and saw a few faces that had that certain look, telling him he had them primed for the kill. "Tomorrow we go to the unholy Rio to stage our protest and I want to see everyone here tomorrow morning at nine o'clock, then we go to cast out the blight that the casino spawns. Are you with me?" He got a moderate response, most of the homeless were asleep or drunk so he counted on the faithful ones who could actually worship. "I'll be here and we'll take the church bus to the sinners and show them we mean business." That got a good response. "Services are now over, go out and do good for God!"

He turned and went to the small rectory off the main church and removed his collar and jacket. He made a call to the Review-Journal newspaper and gave them an anonymous tip about the protest. He wanted people to know he meant business. He then went to his computer and opened up the Twitter home page and studied it for a while longer.

~~*~~

I sat at the computer watching LadyLucky's

twitter stream flashing by. Penny was sitting on a towel on one of the chairs I had for guests in my home office, still wet from her romp in the pool. Willy was on my other chair trying to sleep. Penny was watching the screen as I studied the chatter that went from top to bottom wondering if anyone really paid attention to all this jabbering.

"It's silly to me, I thought Twitter was supposed to be where celebrities would tell people what they were up to, not just one big chat room for everyone from killers to hookers." Penny editorialized.

"I think it has gotten out of hand, everyone promoting or selling or having contests, but there's a lot of good there too. New friends, new people to laugh with. New killers to avoid."

"So you've been at it for about two hours, find out anything?"

"Yeah, Stacey had a lot of admirers. A couple of them are a little whack-a-doodle, otherwise most are just poker freaks who like her attentions. I had one guy send a private message about the sex they had last week, that was a little uncomfortable. I had to study Stacey's past tweets to be able to chat like her."

"At least you're not pretending to be a twelve year old girl looking to pick up pedophiles."

Black Widow Murders

"No I'm a thirty-something woman looking to pick up a serial killer." I laughed.

"I'm going to bed, this is exhausting watching you. Willy and I are leaving you to your foolishness, just don't make any dates with some handsome young man, leave that for me." She picked up a dead looking Willy and took him to the bedroom. I looked at the screen for about another ten minutes, made a few passes at the poker boys, particularly Joe Kepler, the Christian Southern Baptist, who was trash talking sex with me. I wonder what his mother would say if she could see him now. I thought about his connection and wrote a few notes on a pad of paper I had for note taking, I was prepared. I played a bit with Joe then said, screw it, told everyone I had to go, signed off and went to the bedroom.

I was a little stimulated from all the sex talk made by the men, mostly Joe, not that I was interested in men, but the talk was bordering on stimulating one's libido. I was a little worked up myself. Penny was watching me do a little striptease at the foot of the bed and laughed as I stumbled out of my jockey shorts. I jumped on the bed and she closed her eyes and simulated a loud snoring. I just said, "That's all right, I've had sex with you before while you were asleep." She opened one eye and said, "I better not find out that's true."

We had our moment, and then cuddled. Penny was now asleep for real; she could drop off like that. I laid there thinking about the day and wondering who was watching everyone and using it to his advantage. I think I dozed off shortly after.

My cell phone played a tune around five A.M. and I saw it was Deacon. "I hope this is something good, I was having a great sex dream about Pamela Anderson." I felt Penny jab me in the ribs, mumbling that I better not be fooling with her. "What's up?" I asked Deacon.

"We're at the Tabu Bar and we got another body, one guess how he died?"

"It's too early for guessing games; I'll say spiders for $200., Alex."

"Yep, Joe Kepler got it about an hour ago."

I felt a chill and sat up, "Did you say Joe Kepler? The Christian Southern Baptist?"

"Yep, he wasn't exactly practicing his religion at the bar. The killer got him in the john, Kepler was using a stall and found spiders dumped on him while he crapped. There were too many of them for Kepler to fight off and the coroner presumes they started biting when he was trying to brush them off. No witnesses of course."

"Okay I need to meet with you and Lynn about this. Where is Tabu at?" Deacon told me it was in the MGM Grand and I said I'd be there shortly. I hung up and started to dress. Penny mumbled still half asleep, "I better not find out you're going to meet with Pamela Anderson."

"No dear, it's a crime scene; I have some news to share. I'll see you later after your show, call me." I leaned down and kissed her and went out the door.

I arrived at the now closed Tabu Bar about twenty minutes later, and some cop at the door wouldn't let me in, so I called Lynn and she came to rescue me, warning the cop to remember my face. We went in to the restroom where Kepler bought the toilet paper and I got Lynn and Deacon off to the side.

"Okay, I was online pretending to be LadyLucky and guess who was doing some heavy petting with me... or her?"

"Joey boy," Lynn said.

"Yep, he was really laying it on thick about his desires for Stacey. Now he's a victim. Too coincidental for me. Someone on Twitter saw this and went after Kepler. Anything on the cameras around this place?" I asked.

"I got Warren looking at the footage, trying to pick out Kepler in the crowd heading to the john. Do you have a list of who was talking to Stacey... or you or whoever?"

"List won't help, you have to understand that people can lurk in the background and not say anything but still see what others are saying. He could have just watched."

"But how did the killer know Kepler was going to be here?" Deacon asked.

"That's the kicker, Kepler asked Stacey if she wanted to meet him here later, I answered it may be possible, but didn't commit. So that is the only way the killer could have known he was going to be here."

**

Chapter 16

"Where was his protection?" I asked.

"They didn't figure he would have any problems in the can, so they let him go. I now have two detectives who will be cleaning toilets for the next month." Lynn snarled.

"I'm starting to see a connection here. Yesterday Freddie was attacked for the second time after he set up a meeting with Stacey, then this morning Kepler takes a dump, pardon the pun, after he invites her to this club. The focal point has to be Stacey. Someone is jealous of her dalliances on Twitter and is trying to take out the competition." I said.

"So how do we find out who her secret lover is?" Deacon asked.

"Maybe if I take LadyLucky off Twitter for a day or two, he might worry and send a message to her, to find out if she's all right. I'll keep monitoring the thing and hopefully he will make a move."

"I hope he makes a move soon, the Captain warned us there is pressure from above to get this taken care of quickly and quietly, for the WSOP's sake. Now we have another murder and we are only a step closer to finding the killer, Captain's not going to be happy." Lynn said, not smiling.

"Without leads, we have to wait. I'll spend the day watching Twitter, see if he even brags about what he has done. I'm surprised he hasn't sent us a message yet." I said.

"Well, it is only six in the morning, he may be resting from his kill, we may still hear from him yet." Deacon offered.

"So, I'll be in my office today watching my computer, if anyone would like to join me, you know where my office is." I grinned.

"Only too damn well." Lynn said.

~~*~~

Just around nine o'clock the preacher was gathering his signs that he would have his flock carry at the Rio to protest the gambling there. He knew it was a futile attempt, one casino wouldn't yield to his demands, he was in an ocean of gambling and to stop it all would require a nuclear bomb. His motivation was more political. He was going to play to the media, since he called all the television stations to anonymously let them know about the protest and hopefully garner some attention to his cause. He knew his protest wouldn't stop gambling but that wasn't what he was going to be there for.

He came out of the church carrying the signs to hand out to the dozen or so people who actually showed up to support his cause. He herded the followers on to the dilapidated church bus and told the driver to take them to the Rio. The driver grumbled something about lost causes but the preacher didn't hear him over the horrendous noise that the engine made. The bus lurched forward rocking the passengers and made its way down the Boulevard to Flamingo Road and over to the Rio. The bus pulled up to the front of the building and the preacher gave the call to disembark. There were two vans from local television stations sitting out front but that was an everyday occurrence, since celebrities in the WSOP were big news. The preacher hoped they were there for his people. What he didn't know is that they were there to cover the death of a second poker player; they were trying to get a statement from the heads of the WSOP.

The preacher led his people off the wheezing vehicle as the bus driver handed the signs to them. They gathered in the drive of the Rio, as the valet parking attendants watched the people starting to march around the front of the building. One attendant finally called Security and told them of the disturbance.

About three minutes later, Ralph Shay, head of security came walking out with four of his uniformed men. He approached the preacher and said, "Reverend Ben, you've been told before that you can't congregate on the casino property, why do you keep doing this?"

"Ah, Mr. Shay, good to see you again. You know we have a mission to protect the good people of Las Vegas from the devil's disciples," he smiled.

"But why on Rio property, why not go down the street to the MGM or Harrahs to harass them?"

"Because you have the poker tournament here, I must make the statement to the people that this is unacceptable."

"You want to make a statement to the national news, because you know they cover the WSOP. It's a matter of your own press coverage."

"I have to get God's message out to many people, if this is the way, so be it."

"Yeah, well I'm all for freedom of speech, but go do your speech giving on city property. Now move your people back to the sidewalk and I'll leave you alone. I know from past experiences that if I try to get rid of you, it looks bad for the casino. So please go become a problem for the city. I don't want to have to forcibly move you, play nice please."

"Thank you Mr. Shay, God forgives you for working for the heathens."

"Yeah, but God doesn't sign my paycheck. So move it!"

He called for his people to move off the casino property, and then he smiled at Shay and followed. He stood on the side walk wondering if the television crews would be coming out soon to talk to him. He went to his bus driver and asked him quietly to go inside and see where the TV people were and maybe let them know they were out there. The bus driver was told he had to move the bus, so he told the preacher he would after he parked it elsewhere. The preacher said that would be fine, but hurry. The bus driver just thought to himself, "Hurry your own ass," and went off.

~~*~~

I had arrived at the office around ten after running home and finished getting ready for the day, I was in a hurry to get to the crime scene this morning so I passed on my morning shower and two pieces of toast. Penny had already gone off to do her show, and Lacey had picked up Willy, so I had the place to myself before I drove to the office. I came in the entrance and Willy started bouncing over to greet me. I picked him up and said good morning to Lacey, she smiled and returned the greeting. I asked if Buck was in, she said he was, I went into the hallway to his office and he was leaning back watching a smaller TV he had brought in.

"Watching soaps?" I asked.

"Nope, there's a report on now about some local preacher and his flock protesting the WSOP at the Rio. He seems like a man determined to let people know where he stands about gambling," Buck said.

I stood and watched for a few minutes and said I'd be in my office most the day watching Twitter for any clues to my murders. He grunted and went on watching the breaking news story.

Bob Moats

I opened my door and put Willy on the client chair; he plopped down and watched me. I sat at the desk and picked up the remote and turned on the LCD TV I had brought out from Michigan when we moved, and put the thing in my office to watch Penny's new talk show. She wasn't on yet as I woke my computer from it's sleep and clicked the Twitter icon. It took a few seconds to recognize the cookie in the computer that said I was LadyLucky and open the home page. I turned the channel to the protest and watched a few minutes as the reporter was talking to some preacher.

"Reverend Ben, do you really think your protest will put a dent in the World Series of Gambling's tournament here at the Rio?" The crafty reporter asked.

"I don't think our small group will actually do much, but we are counting on the good Christians out there to join our fight against the devil's tools. If we can show that David can slay Goliath again, then we are doing our work for God. I even have waged a campaign on the social media site Twitter to get our cause across." The preacher was in his glory now.

I thought about his comment about him being on Twitter and when it was ready I typed in the search box the name Reverend Ben. After digging through its files the screen name popped up, RevBen, and I clicked on the name bringing up his profile page. Sure enough, he was rallying people to tear down the walls of gambling and rise up against the heathens who promote it. He had a surprisingly good number of followers, probably people curious to see what the nut job had to say. I scanned down his tweets that he had posted in the last couple days and it was basically the same stuff.

I've heard it a thousand times before on local TV as I scanned the channels looking for something to watch on a Sunday morning. Every Tele-Evangelist preaching to the flock about the evils of this and that. Those faithful flocks of people put on blinders when it came to life, they'd be shocked if they went into the seedier parts of their own towns to see what actually goes on. Drugs, prostitution, gang fighting just to name a few, not to leave out what goes on in the privacy of people's homes, wife beating, child endangerment, and even molesting children. Good Christians are even involved in most of these daily occurrences. Damn hypocrites.

I stopped going through his tweets when I saw it. He had mentioned LadyLucky in one tweet, talked to her a couple of lines, so I went to LadyLucky's private messages and scrolled down until I found what I was looking for, messages from Reverend Ben, and they were slightly sexual. I called Lynn.

**

Chapter 17

Lynn and Deacon were in my office again. Lynn was looking to the side of my room sizing it up for her desk, she joked. I pulled out the printout I made from the tweets between Stacey and Reverend Ben, Lynn was studying them with Deacon looking over her shoulder. I often wondered how Deacon felt being in Lynn's shadow, she always taking the lead and he following. I did finally ask him one day and he said he wasn't bothered by it, he was let off the hook for decisions that he'd rather not make. He liked his job and he loved Lynn so he kept his job and personal life separate.

"As you can see, the remarks from RevBen were innuendos but suggestive. Not something a minister would say to someone. I'm surprised he would do something like this knowing it could come back at him. I'd put him at the top of my list of suspects for the killings. I'm still going to watch the stream of tweets just in case, you can do what you want with him, just keep me informed so I don't go nuts sitting here reading all this garbage," I said.

Lynn smiled and said they'd go visit RevBen and see what he had to say. I waved to them as they left and went back to peeping on people. I used to lurk a lot on Twitter when I first signed up, just to see what it was all about. Then I started to get to know a number of people who were writers or interested in writing, and they liked to be seen with a published Best Selling author. Then it got boring and I found myself spending too much time there and not working on my new books, so I just lurked until I grew tired of it all, too much chatter and not enough progress. In the last couple months I had just stayed away altogether.

I still had on the picture of the news reports about the slaying of a second poker player, but had the sound off. I turned it back on to listen to the second hand account of the killings, they were slightly twisted. Amazing being in on a murder investigation and listening to what the media says about it. Like it was two different cases. I wondered how slanted or misinformed our news media actually was, and how much should we accept.

I heard the front door bell tinkle and could hear mumbling in the lobby. I stood and went to the hallway and looked out to the reception counter and saw it was Penny with some bags in hand. She put them on the counter as Lacey came over to watch her open them. I came out after talking Willy down from his chair and came up behind Penny and blew on her neck. I had to duck as she came around with her arm ready to belt me.

"Hey watch it; you could put someone's eye out with that arm," I yelled but softly.

"You're lucky I didn't pull my .38 and shoot you. I'm still leery about spiders and you blowing on my neck doesn't help," she replied.

I looked around her to see what she had in the bags, it was pastries. She smiled and said she had on a pastry chef from the Hilton's Steakhouse Restaurant on her show today showing how to make various pastries and there were samples left over after she held off the stage crew. She told us to help ourselves after she called Buck out.

We celebrated with the sweets and I had to unbuckle my belt a bit after the third custard crème, they were better than Krispy Kremes. Penny sat in my client chair with Willy on her lap as I watched the Twitter stream whiz by.

"So what does the preacher do for Stacey?" she asked.

"I don't know and I need to call Lynn to ask Stacey how far the familiarity went. But I'm afraid to call Lynn right now; she's probably getting tired of me," I said as my phone rang, it was Lynn. I looked to Penny and said, "well the mountain is coming to me."

"Hello, found out anything interesting?" I put the phone on speaker.

"Well, we pulled in Reverend Ben and he's

dancing around with bible in hand. I threatened him with the tweets he made between him and LadyLucky, but he just quoted bible phrases and ignored the conversation. He's good at avoiding confrontation. I talked to Stacey about him and she says he's harmless."

"Yeah, and they said John Wayne Gacy was a funny clown, but he tortured, raped and murdered 33 men. Did Stacey ever meet up with RevBen?"

"She said she wasn't interested in him, since he was against poker in all forms. So I'm not sure he's a likely suspect. How's the peeping going?"

"I'm dying here; no one is worrying about LadyLucky being missing in action. Where's RevBen now?"

"He's still interrogation. I was hoping you might have some new news for me."

"Sorry, you got all I got. Does RevBen know Stacey is in jail?"

"No we haven't mentioned it to anyone, we figured it might mess up your stake out," she laughed.

"Thanks, this stake out is killing me."

"Now you know how cops feel sitting watching a suspect all night."

"Yep, I have to hand it to their perseverance. Keep me informed and I'll do the same."

"Okay, I'll talk later." She said and hung up.

~~*~~

Lynn went back to interrogation and stood looking at the Reverend, "You are on top of my suspect list for murder of the WSOP poker players. You haven't been candid about your distaste for them, and you've said everything short of murder in your rants about them." She waited for him to speak.

"I don't have to murder; I use the word of God to bring down the walls of evil. You should look elsewhere, I know nothing about these killings and I don't like spiders." He sat back with a smirk.

"Okay, Reverend, get out of here. I will be watching you, so be aware." She turned to the cop guarding him and said, "Show our guest to the front door."

"Excuse me, but how do I get home, you people brought me here?" he asked before Lynn could leave.

"Ask your God to get you home," Lynn said

tersely, then told the guard to get him a ride and stormed out.

Deacon and Warren were relaxing in observation as Lynn came in. "I don't like that man. He's pompous and arrogant. I want a team on him at all times, follow his every move. Warren, take care if it."

He said he would and went out. Lynn sat in his vacated chair and put her head on Deacon's shoulder. "Careful, you're fraternizing with a fellow officer," Deacon said to the top of her head.

"I don't care, I've just about had it with murder and spiders and religious drumbeaters. I'm cutting Stacey loose under the condition that she stays off Twitter till we get something, or I'll haul her back in for the solicitation charges. I hope Jim finds something soon; the Captain was giving me the evil eye this morning. I'm happy he didn't chew me out."

"He's got other things on his mind, I heard him complaining about his new girlfriend giving him a hard time." Deacon smiled.

"Weber has a girlfriend?" Lynn asked.

"Yep, met her through a friend, it was a blind date."

"She'd have to be blind to date Weber." Lynn laughed.

"Careful, you know Weber has great hearing."

"Let's get out of here and go bug Jim and Penny for a while. I'm beginning to like Jim's office."

They stood and went out of observation, Lynn telling Warren they were going to follow up on a few leads, lying to him, but she didn't care.

~~*~~

Penny still had pastries left over when Lynn and Deacon arrived. They both indulged in the sweet treats and we all sat in my office relaxing as I kept an eye on the computer screen.

"RevBen has my vote for these murders, but we need to prove it," Lynn spoke after finishing off a crème puff.

"Well, we'll see if he gets on Twitter to make any statements," I offered.

"I had them release Stacey with a warning that she stay off Twitter until we find something to go with. She says she doesn't want to screw up Harvey's insurance policy beneficiary payout. That woman is still on my list of suspects," Lynn said licking the crème goo from her fingers.

135

Black Widow Murders

"She had motive and opportunity to hire someone to kill her husband, but the attempt on Freddie and then Kelper's murder makes me wonder why she would go on with this. She could have stopped after the attempt on Freddie to divert attention from Harvey's murder."

"I'm still not understanding the spider aspect of it. Poison, gun, knife, anything, but why spiders?" Deacon said.

"Well here's something. RevBen just came on Twitter and made a post about how the police are all tools of the casinos. I'm reading, 'They couldn't find their killer so they pick on me, waste of people's taxes.' and he goes on to say, 'They look away from the real criminals to innocent people.' The rest is just rants about the WSOP and the police are in their pockets."

"I am so not liking that man," Lynn growled.

"Well, RevBen is at it again, he says he sent a private message to LadyLucky. Hold on while I change screens to see what he wants to say." I clicked on the Direct Message button and it came up with Stacey's private messages. "I'm reading, '@LadyLucky Lady, be careful they are onto you.' That's all he says."

**

Chapter 18

"Why did the good Reverend do that when he knows you have evidence that he conversed with Stacey. Wouldn't he try to stay away?" I asked as I watched for any further posts.

"Maybe he had no other way to contact her other than twitter," Deacon offered.

"I'm going to ask him," I said. Reading out loud as I typed, "What do you mean?" I asked, then I clicked the send button and waited for a reply.

Lynn was watching over my shoulder as we waited and said, "He's not going to reply, he was just sending a warning. He doesn't figure we would see just one small post."

"Nope, here it comes, he says, '@LadyLucky Not now, meet same place'." That's all he said, I waited to see more. "If I ask where they meet he may get suspicious, you need to question Stacey again, and this time she needs to do a little talking."

I was still watching the Twitter stream when I saw it. "Oh hell, look at this!" I pointed to one line it said, "@RevBen can't meet. Talk later." It was from Stacey. "Damn, she got on and she's screwing up our stake out."

Lynn got on her cell and called Warren, when he came on she said to pull Stacey Trent back in ASAP. She hung up and came back to me as I was starting to send a private message from my own twitter account. "@LadyLucky What the hell are you doing, you were told to stay off Twitter!"

Lynn said not to send it. "It may frighten her off, Warren is on the way." She turned to Deacon and said, "Let's get back and wait for her. I hope she's doing this from her own computer and not some internet café." She turned to me and continued, "Keep watching and keep me informed." They left.

Penny sat in my client chair and said, "So this kind of sets up the two of them for pulling something?"

"Well, it doesn't look good for them now. It shows they have something going, it could be murder. Stacey wants her husband's insurance money and the good reverend wants to cast out evil. They feed off each other. The thing I'm wondering about now, he said to Stacey that they were on to her, but Lynn told me she didn't say much to him about Stacey other than his tweets to her. What did he believe they were on to her about, the murder or his dalliances with her? I hope Lynn can get something out of her now."

"Well, I'm hungry, want a sandwich?" Penny smiled and stood.

"After all those pastries? Are you buying?" I asked.

"Sure, with your money," she said as she held out her hand. I grinned and pulled a twenty out of my pocket and gave it to her.

"Get me my usual. See what Lacey and Buck want."

"Be back shortly," she said and went out.

I heard the front door bell tinkle as Penny went out. I had told her to park in the front, not the back; at least until the spider killer was caught. I didn't really feel he would go after Penny, but it's better to be safe. I watched the screen but wasn't seeing anything more from either of the idiots online. I saw a few people I knew so sent them a couple messages just to have something sane to do. I saw Freddie and sent him a private message about not discussing the case. He said he wouldn't, but was getting antsy about the finals coming up the day after tomorrow. I thought about that, the killer would have to start moving if he was going to attempt any more kills, but what if he had accomplished his goal. Although Freddie was still alive after two attempts. I sent him a message to stay away from talking to LadyLucky; he agreed that he wanted nothing to do with the psycho.

About twenty minutes later, Penny came back with the sandwiches and handed them out. She came back to my office and gave me my ham and Swiss on rye and sat. "Where's my change?" I asked.

"It was a tip for the delivery person," she smiled. I couldn't argue with her logic.

Willy was circling the front of the desk waiting for his share of the food, Penny pulled out a small finger sandwich she got for him and put it on a paper plate she got from our supply closet. He ate in tiny bites enjoying himself. Penny sat in the client chair and unwrapped her sandwich as I checked mine to see if they put on mustard and not mayo.

My cell rang, it was Lynn, I answered and she told me they couldn't find Stacey but she had Reverend Ben pulled back in. She asked if I would come in to hear the questioning in case there were some twitter details she may not know about. I looked at my sandwich, barely touched and said I'd be in.

I stood, wrapping the sandwich back up and put it in my office cube fridge and then said to Penny, "I have to go help the police do their job. I'll be back whenever, if you're not here, then I'll see you at home. Why don't you invite Lacey over to swim and relax, I'd feel safer if you had company."

"That sounds good, I'll ask her, but my favorite company is my .38 and it talks loud." She laughed. I said, "But the .38 doesn't swim very well."

She stood and kissed me good-bye as I left the office and went out the front door.

I started up the Crown Vic and drove out to Tropicana and over to Metro headquarters. On the way I was trying to put everything together that I had seen or heard since Lynn first asked if I liked spiders. I had nothing against them, but wondered why the killer bothered to use them? Was it for fun, drama, or just had a lot of handy spiders in his house and found a way to get rid of them. The RevBen and LadyLucky thing really had me going. What was Ben's warning about; he had something to tell her. Oh well, with Reverend Ben back in for questioning maybe Lynn could shake him loose. I pulled into the Metro lot and parked.

I came in the back entrance of Metro and found Lynn and Deacon standing in the hallway by interrogation. "I knew you couldn't do this without me."

"Did they have to widen the back door for you to get in the building with that head?" Deacon asked.

"Yes, after they raised it so you wouldn't have to duck to get in," I said.

Black Widow Murders

Deacon laughed out loud and Lynn gave us both an evil look, so we just shut up. She turned to me and said, "I want you in the room with me so you can refute anything he may say about the online business. He probably thinks I don't understand it, which I don't. So we need to work together on this."

I said it was no problem and she went to the door. We walked in as Reverend Ben just sat staring at the mirror. He didn't acknowledge us as we sat across from him. He then looked to me and smiled. "Peace be with you brother," he said.

"I'm not your brother and I make my own peace, thank you," I said back.

His eyebrows raised slightly and he looked to Lynn, "Is he going to be the bad cop?"

"He's not a cop, he's a civilian advisor. This is Jim Richards, our advisor for computer related help and a private investigator who was hired by Stacey Trent to find her husband's killer. You don't know anything about Harvey Trent's murder do you?"

"Should I?" Reverend Ben gave a blank look; he had acting abilities that are befitting of an evangelist.

"Come on Rev, you sent a warning message to

Stacey, her husband was murdered and we think you know more than you tell. What were you warning her about, that you couldn't tell her without a meeting?"

He sat quietly, "I was going to warn her that you may have knowledge of our trysts. We were keeping our affair quiet, until the murder was solved."

"Stacey told us she had nothing to do with you."

"What would you expect her to say, I was banging the preacher while my husband was being murdered."

That statement made me perk up. "So you were with Stacey the night of Harvey's murder?" I asked before Lynn could.

"Yes, we decided not to tell anyone, our love for each other was to be kept secret until this all blew over."

Lynn leaned forward to him and said, "Your love for each other? Did you know she was banging other men, the poker players who were being murdered? Maybe you got jealous and decided to get rid of the competition."

"I know nothing of these other men, she wouldn't do that."

"Well, we hauled her in for solicitation when she tried to take Freddie Norris, a poker player, to bed for money. How's that for a lover, Rev?"

He sat thinking, his eyes darting back and forth. He started to look irritated and banged his fist on the table causing Lynn and I to jump. "I wondered if she was fucking around with those damn poker players, her little messages to them that I couldn't read. She would say she was just getting information on her husband's faithfulness, she told me she thought he was screwing around and the other players were her way to find out. Damn whore!"

Well, that put a new light on the case, I thought.

**

Chapter 19

"Talk to me, Rev, was Stacey involved in these killings?" Lynn asked.

"I don't know, really, I don't. We didn't talk much about them. She said it was a terrible thing, but she didn't want to dwell on it. She stopped loving her husband and even grew to dislike him for his addiction to gambling."

"How did you get involved with her?"

"We first met on Twitter, and then we ran into each other at one of my church functions to cast out gambling from Vegas. We were protesting in front of the Flamingo Hotel before they chased us off. She was against gambling since it ruined her marriage, saw us and said she happened to be in the area we were protesting, and stopped to talk to me. We went out for coffee and talked for hours, she was quite a woman. We had our first... well, we were together for the first time that night her husband was murdered. She said she wouldn't tell anyone who she was with." He went quiet, looking to the table in front of him. We gave him the space. "She said I was special, she could get used to my way of life, fighting against gambling."

"Why are you so against gambling since you are in the gambling Mecca of the world? You can't stop it, what did you think you would accomplish?" I asked.

"I have my reasons, I'm realistic about the fact I can't fight it, I just needed a platform and exposure to get my church built up. You see I have this dream of having my own Crystal Cathedral and my own television show preaching the word to millions."

Black Widow Murders

"And making millions," Lynn said.

"I'm not a fool, I know there is money to be made, but first I was trying to build up my following."

"You know if Stacey gets her insurance money, two million dollars, that would be a good start to help build your empire wouldn't it?" I asked.

He looked to me confused, "Two millions dollars from Harvey's death?"

"You're saying that you didn't know about his life insurance policy?" Lynn asked.

"No, I didn't. She never said anything about it."

"Just what did she tell you?"

"She told me she wanted to be with me because she liked my beliefs and when Harvey was murdered, she was broken up but didn't mention anything about money. I figured since he was dead, she would have no money since he lost most of his funds gambling, at least that's what she told me."

"Well, she's been lying and withholding information from a lot of people. Do you know where we can find her; she seems to be in the wind?" Lynn asked.

"No, I don't, she has her apartment in the city

but I've never been there. She had no friends that she told me about, but now I wonder what else she lied to me about." He went quiet again, staring at his reflection in the mirror.

"Where did you and Stacey stay together the night Harvey was murdered and what times were you there?" Lynn asked knowing the answer, but testing him.

"We went to the Wayfarer Motel, room 24. I was there from about eight P.M. and Stacey came around nine, I think. We were in all night then she left around six in the morning. We stayed in all night; she never left the room, so she couldn't have killed her husband."

"You do know that Harvey was murdered using Black Widow spiders?"

"I had heard he was bitten by a spider, strange way to kill someone, so unpredictable."

"What do you mean unpredictable?" Lynn asked.

"Those spiders have to be upset or annoyed to bite, you have to coax them, and only the females will bite. If they were put on Harvey, someone would have had to get them stirred up, blow on them or brush them with a feather, spiders hate birds."

Black Widow Murders

"You know a lot about them?"

"I had a course in entomology when I attended UNLV back ten years ago. Black Widows were part of the course since they are prevalent in this area."

"Do you know anyone who might raise them or have access to a lot of them?"

"No I don't, I was never fond of spiders, and I avoid them when I can."

"Okay, Rev, I'm letting you go for now, but if we see you on Twitter or talking to Stacey again, you will be pulled back in for obstruction of justice, or conspiracy for murder. You make it your choice, now get lost." Lynn stood and motioned to me to follow; I did as we went out.

We stood in the squad room just outside the interrogation room as Deacon came out of observation. I said, "I hope RevBen isn't pissed enough to go out and murder Stacey now."

Lynn smiled and said, "Well, it would solve two problems, getting rid of Stacey and putting Ben away. But I didn't say that."

We all went quiet as Ben was being taken out of interrogation by a uniformed cop, Lynn called to the cop and said to have a car take him home, and they went out the front entrance. Warren was just coming down the back hallway, Lynn called him over, "Any word on Stacey yet?"

"Nope, she's invisible. I got men watching her apartment and a guy watching her credit cards for activity. She makes a move, we'll know."

We were standing there when I heard a familiar voice from behind us saying, "You guys could have at least put up a welcome home banner." I turned to see who spoke and was shocked to see Will Trapper. "Don't I get a big kiss from anyone?" he laughed.

We all went to him and Lynn spoke, "What are you doing here, and does Captain Weber know?"

"I just got done talking to him in his office. We've buried the hatchet and he's not pressing charges for all the pranks I pulled on him last time I was here. But he did say he was going to have me watched carefully though."

I held my hand out to shake and asked, "How's Barry and Earl?"

"They're both fine. Becker is now in charge of cold cases, he'll be ready for homicide in a few years, but he said he's patient. Earl is still in your office and Paula is still his receptionist and secretary. He has been busy with cases so he's happy. Me, I've retired from the force and I'm moving back home to Vegas."

Black Widow Murders

That news hit me. "Wow, have you moved yet, or just here looking for a place to live?" I asked.

"I'm moving into my old childhood home, Mom never sold the place and the renters are moving out with a little persuasion," he said happily.

"Did you use your gun or just tell them there were termites in the house?" Deacon asked, glad to see his old boss again.

"I told them the house would be haunted by me if they didn't find another place to go. Besides, they were way behind on their rent and it didn't look like they were going to pay it anytime soon. As soon as they are out, I'll fumigate and move in. Buck still alive?"

"Yep, he's got a security guard business going out of our office here. What are you going to do now that you're back?"

"Well, I have a pension from the police, and I've started the paperwork to get my private license out here, do you need a partner on the west coast?" He grinned like he was expecting me to say no.

"You started the paperwork, how long have you been out here?" Lynn asked.

"About three days, I've been looking up old friends and calling in some favors from my old cop buddies. So do I have a place to hang my shingle?" he smiled at me.

"I'd be honored to have you busting crime with us, just like old times," I said.

"Great, I got to see an old friend in the county building who is working up my license forms then I'll get back with you. Still got the same phone number?"

"Yep, same one."

"Good, I have some errands to run, if it's okay, I'd like to see your new home."

"Penny will be happy to see you; tonight we'll all gather at our house and burn some meat on the incinerator."

"I love it, good to see all of you again, I'll be back." He said and went out through the front way.

"Now there's a surprise," I said.

"A good one," Deacon offered.

"Guys, let's get our minds back on the case," Lynn said.

"What case is that, oh yes, the spiders," I said with an evil face and a growl. Lynn gave me a dirty look and walked away. "Think I offended her?" I asked Deacon.

"Yep, she's not going to like you now."

We all met outside Lynn's office as Warren came up behind us. "Got a small lead on Stacey, she was spotted sneaking out the back of her apartment by the guys on stake out, but they just missed her and she got away. They did get the make of the car and have a BOLO out. We'll get her," he said and went off.

~~*~~

The man had just come out of the room from gathering his pets. He put the container on his workbench and took off his protective suit. He went to the computer and read the private messages he had read about a half hour ago. He was surprised to see them and smiled, he knew his next victim.

**

Chapter 20

I said to Lynn that I wanted to do some investigating on my own, "maybe if we split up, something will turn up quicker."

"Sounds like a plan, just keep me informed and give us a call about that B-B-Q at your place," Lynn said.

I said my good-byes and went out to my car and sat for a minute, pulling out my cell phone and called Penny. She came on and I said, "Hey babe, guess who's in town?"

"The Pope?" she replied.

"Close, Trapper is moving here and he surprised us with a visit at the precinct. I invited him, Lynn and Deacon over for a barbecue tonight to celebrate his return to Vegas."

"Wow, Trapper is back in town, does Weber know?"

"He does and they're on friendly terms now. So is a B-B-Q in the cards?"

"Sounds good to me, I'll invite Buck and Lacey and we'll make it a party. Do we have enough meat for them?"

"I'll pick some up on my way home, figure about seven o'clock." We finished up with a bit of mushy talk and I hung up as I drove out of Metro parking.

I headed the Crown Vic over to the Rio Hotel. On the way I was reviewing everything I heard from the good reverend and wondered if Stacey could have hired someone to kill her husband or was she just an unwitting player in this dangerous game.

I called Mac and told him I was coming up and he said he'd watch for me. I parked, went into the lobby and over to the elevators riding up to the tenth floor again. Mac opened the door after I knocked and he peeped through the hole.

"Hey big guy, all quiet here?" I asked.

"Yep, Freddie is sleeping in the bedroom, rough night gambling, and Dontae is taking a shower. This hotel living is nice, I could get used to this," he said with a grin.

I went to the bedroom and saw a covered lump that was Freddie, sleeping peacefully on the huge king-sized bed. I went up to him and yelled, "Hey, time to get up!!"

His eyes went wide and he sat up like a bolt and looked around until he saw me standing next to him. "Damn man, don't do that, I'm jumpy enough."

"Well, get up and come out to the other room, and please get dressed, I don't need to see you in the flesh," I said since I now noticed he was naked when he threw off the silk sheet. I went out of the bedroom and over to the room service cart covered with snacks and food still fresh. I helped myself to some cheese and crackers thinking about the ham and cheese sandwich still in my office fridge wondering if I would ever get to it.

Mac came up and grabbed a few chips and said, "It's been quiet here since the last attempt, I've been watching all the openings in the room for spider attacks and checking anything coming into the room."

"Great; Buck will have to start a bodyguard service also, it would be useful for taking care of all the celebrities who come into town."

"I'd like that, I would love to guard a few movie starlets like Lindsey or maybe a singer like Shania Twain."

"The country singer, she has beautiful eyes," I said.

"Yeah, and her other parts aren't bad either," he laughed.

"I was referring to those other parts," I smiled.

Freddie came out only wearing his khaki shorts again, I looked to Mac and he just shrugged and made a resigned look.

"Freddie, tell me about Stacey, everything you know and also everything you know about Harvey."

Black Widow Murders

He staggered over to the bar and poured himself a scotch straight up; I cringed wondering how anyone could drink hard liquor this early. He gulped it down, poured another and went to the couch. "Stacey, AKA LadyLucky, started hanging around the guys on twitter after we got into town. I guess since she lived here, she figured it would be easy to hit on us, which she did. I don't have any word from the other players whether she spent the night with anyone, like she attempted with me, but I was sure she had some contact. I just figured her for a poker groupie, not the wife of one of the players. Poor Harvey." He stopped to take a drink and continued, "Harvey was an odd duck, really quiet and smart. I think he had a good memory for the cards, and it helped him be the best of all of us."

"So you think he would have taken the tourney?"

"Yeah, he was in a good position and was smoking hot with the cards. I really think he would have made it. But that's neither here nor there now is it."

"All modesty aside, how do you rank the players now?"

"I'd say with all due modesty, I am in a better position now with Harvey gone. Oh and Joe Kepler is out now that he's dead, he would have been next, then Mathew Langer, he's real good. Harold

Carlisle and Sara Feinman were about equal, but I'd bet on Sara to beat Harold."

"Okay, so the ranks go from Harvey, you, Kepler, Langer, Carlisle and Feinman?"

"Well I'd put Sara above Carlisle, but yeah, that's pretty much how I would bet on it."

"So Harvey is dead, along with Kepler, and two attempts have been made on you, sounds like someone is killing off the great chefs of Europe."

Freddie looked at me strange like, I said, "It was an old movie about chefs being murdered... never mind, you had to be there. So the top of the crop are being murdered. Do they have alternates who fill in for the vacant seats?"

"I don't know, we've never had murders before, so I guess it's up to the tournament officials whether they fill the board. But I would venture a guess that they'd just let the survivors battle it out."

"Do you ever bet on yourself or other players at the sports book in the casinos?"

"Yeah, I've placed small wagers, it would be dumb not to, especially when you're close to the source."

"Wouldn't that be like insider trading, do they allow it?"

"Well, they don't like it and the rules say you're not supposed to, but we all do it. As long as no one complains. Besides, we don't bet at the sports book, too close to being seen. We use the bookies that operate under the law, less chance to be outed."

"Do you know if any of your opponents have placed any wagers?"

"I wouldn't tell them if I did, so figure they wouldn't tell me. Like I said it's not something you want everyone to know."

"Who's your bookie, may I ask?"

"No, I'm not giving out that information, he has very strict rules about telling on him and he has some very big enforcers to be sure we don't."

"Okay Freddie, good luck in the tournament. Mac, can I talk to you outside?" I said as I headed to the door followed by Mac.

I stopped outside the door and turned to him, "Penny and I are having a barbecue tonight with Lacey and all the gang, to welcome a friend who just moved here from Michigan, you're invited too. Call Buck to send a relief for you, tell him I said so. We'll be starting about seven, you know where the house is, hope you can make it." He said that would be nice to see Lacey again. I told him we'd see him later and left.

I got to my car and sat thinking about how to find a few bookies and not get beat up. I could face a lot of dangerous things if it was thrown at me, but I'm not a really brave person when it came to putting my neck out. I pulled my phone and called Deacon, he came on after the third ring.

"Anything new on the crime front?" I asked.

"Not since you left here almost an hour ago."

"I need some info, are you free to talk about illegal matters?"

"Yeah, I'm in the break room, I'm alone. What's up?"

"Do you know any bookies that don't work for the casinos?"

"I've been on a couple vice strikes, but those guys are all little fish, do you need the big hitters?"

"Yeah, one's that would take huge bets on the WSOP."

"I can't help you but I know someone who may, if he's still available. You remember Don Mason from our last crime wave?"

"Yeah, the cop who was caught for fudging murder reports?"

"The very one, he only ended up in a bad situation with Muldoon and his crew because he was betting heavy and loosing. He may know where the big fish are at."

"Works for me, you got an address or contact number?"

Deacon said to hold on and then I could hear him banging the phone around. He came back, "Got something to write on?"

I had already gotten my pad of paper and pen I keep in the car, so I was ready and said so, he gave me an address and I wrote it down. I reminded him of the time for our party tonight.

"Lynn and I are getting Trapper a big bouquet of balloons to put up at your house, so we'll be there a little earlier if that's all right?"

"No problem, I have to call Will and tell him how to get to the house, so we'll have time to decorate."

"Thanks, see you then and good luck with Mason." He hung up and I put my phone back in my pocket. I took out my Palm TX and opened the map program that I would be lost without. I found Mason's place of residence, I wasn't sure if it was a house or apartment, but Deacon didn't mention an apartment number so I assumed it to be a house. I started the Crown Vic and drove out of the Rio Parking and over to Durango and up to Cheyenne. I found the house, it wasn't the best house on the block, and it looked like it was built back when the city first started to build up. I went to the door and knocked. Mason opened the door, looked at me with blood shot eyes and said, "What do you want Richards?"

**

Chapter 21

At least he remembered me from when Deacon and I went to visit him at North Vegas PD precinct about Lacey's supposed murder case. It was the only time I met him; later it came out that while he was the investigating detective, he falsified case reports of the murder to cover for the criminals he was involved with. He fell into working for them because he had owed money he didn't have for gambling debts to bookies. I hoped he would be open enough to share who his bookies were.

"You remember me?"

"Yeah, it's because of your nosing around trying to find out what happened with Lacey Lee, I got caught and my girlfriend was murdered. Sure I remember you," he said distastefully.

I just stood there, I was sorry for the man but he brought it on himself, I didn't make him break the law. "I'm sorry for your loss, but you would have been caught eventually, even if I hadn't been following the leads. And it was Willis who ratted you out."

He stood looking at me then he gave a sigh, shook his head and said, "Yeah, I can't blame anyone else for my troubles but me. I screwed up and I took the heat. At least I'm not in prison, if I hadn't dug up all the evidence on the bad guys and kept it safely away, I'd be pissing in cell. What do you want?"

"Can I speak to you about gambling, purely for informational purposes?"

He stood staring again, "I guess so, come on in." He walked away from the door and disappeared around a corner. I slowly entered hoping he wasn't going for a weapon. I braced myself as I heard him coming back, but all he had a drink glass in hand with a brown liquid filling it half up. He motioned to me and I followed him to his kitchen where he pointed to a chair at his table. "Want a drink?" he asked.

"No thanks, too early for me."

"What about gambling you need to know?"

"I'm working on a case for a woman whose husband was murdered the other day."

"Was he the poker player bit by spiders?"

"Yes, he was. Harvey Trent."

"Oh, you don't have to tell me his name. I used to bet on him and win, then my luck went south and I got cocky picking the wrong people to bet on."

"Harvey and Joe Kepler both were murdered and Freddie Norris had two attempts on his life, I'm working for Trent's wife to find his killer."

"Kepler dead too? Damn shame, he would have been awesome if he kept his dick in his pants."

"Have you ever heard of or met Trent's wife Stacey?"

"LadyFucky? Sure, she was popular around the poker circuit. Everyone knew her but Harvey, and I mean that in the biblical sense. She laid more pipe than a plumber. If you want to look for a murderer, look to her, she hated her husband." He took a swig from his drink, made a face. "Damn cola doesn't taste the same since they screwed with the formula. I've been sober now ever since May was killed. She was always pushing me to quit, I just didn't do it when she was alive, now I don't drink to serve her memory. You got a good woman Richards, don't lose her."

"Penny is strong and able to take care of herself, but I worry about her all the time. Too many nutcases out there."

"Damn straight. Now what did you want to know about gambling?"

"Well, I have a theory I'm working on, it involves heavy betting on the WSOP players."

"That goes on all the time, even when they aren't in town, the tourney goes on all over the country."

"I'm talking about the players themselves betting."

"Ah, a no-no if you are a competitor. So you're talking bookies under the radar?"

"Yeah, I need a few names so I can see if any of the players have put down heavy bets on the outcome."

"Murder off a few of the key players and narrow the odds, I get that. I can give you a few leads, but you didn't get them from me. Understand?"

"My lips are sealed."

Mason stood and went to a drawer at his kitchen counter, pulling out a pad of paper and pencil. He came back to the table and was busy writing down some names. He finished and tore the page off and handed it to me.

"Between us, understand?"

"You got my word."

"You most likely won't get much cooperation from these guys, and they have some heavy hitters behind them, they break bones and don't care. Be careful and take an army with you."

He took another drink and smiled. "I miss being a cop. It was my life, and I screwed it up. Gambling was something I couldn't get away from. May tried to get me to give it up, but it took her death to make me see the light as they say."

"Do you know a Reverend Ben?"

"Yeah, he's creepy and only out for himself. We hauled him in a few times up in North Vegas for drunk and disorderly back when he was just a minor street preacher, but he got street cred with the indigent people and started his mission. He pulled them in; they came and believed in his crap, enough to make a small name around town. I do believe if given the chance he could be powerful. Don't trust him, whatever you do."

Black Widow Murders

"Do you think he's capable of murder?"

"Mr. God, oh hell no. He's the kind of Svengali who guides people to do bad things; he wouldn't soil his holy hands to do the devil's work. If you are looking to him for Trent's murder, I'd look to his followers, they would do just about anything for him."

I thought about that, "Reverend Ben established a relationship with Stacey and her husband turns up dead, but what would be his motive?"

"Reverend Ben and Stacey? That's a good one. She couldn't stand him from what I heard, he was dead against card games and she got her jollies from the players. Who told you he and she were involved?"

"The good reverend told us today, he said Stacey was in love with him and they were going to start a new religious order." I half joked.

"Well, I'd take that for what it's worth, not much. We had the reverend under suspicion for murders when we found out that a few homeless people were taking out insurance policies and naming his church as beneficiary. Those homeless would be found dead from exposure to the heat or killed by hit and run. We just couldn't pin it on him, he always had an alibi. The killings stopped and we were busy with other cases, so he was put on the back burner. Watch out for him."

"Well, you've given me more than I expected," I said as I looked to my watch realizing I had little time to get the meat for the barbecue. "I have to go; Penny and I are hosting a welcome back to Vegas party for an old friend tonight. You may have heard of him, he was kind of a legend around Vegas police, Will Trapper?"

"Will Trapper, hell yeah; I was in police academy with him. After that I went to North Vegas Police and he went to Metro. He was insane back then, I especially liked that he would bring hookers into the cells for the precinct guys. He racked up a lot of favors from them over that. He could run this town on just the blackmail stuff he accumulated."

I laughed at the thought, finding out more about my friend and his past. "You were friends?"

"Yeah, we ran together for a number of years, until he moved to Michigan. Lost touch with him."

I had a thought, "Why don't you come by the house tonight to join us, Trapper may get a kick out of seeing you. And you can fill in Lynn Carter on Reverend Ben's past. Sound all right?"

"Yeah, I'd like that. Thanks," he said with a smile. I took his pad of paper and wrote down the address and told him to come around seven, he said he'd be there and walked me to the door.

"Richards, you're an okay guy, sorry I misjudged you."

"No problem, I'm sorry for your troubles. See you later." I said and went to my car.

I sat as I remembered that I had to call Trapper to give him the address, so I pulled out my cell and called the old number of his cell phone I had for him, hoping it still worked. It rang a couple times and I heard his voice saying with a laugh, "What do you want now Richards?" I laughed remembering how many times he would say that when I would call for a favor or information.

"Where are you at?"

"I'm reminiscing with a couple of friends in the bicycle street patrol; I'm on the strip and found them standing around eating croissants. Damn high class cops, can't eat plain old donuts. You do have the meat for the barbecue?"

"I'm working on it; I just called to give you the address."

"I got it already; I am still a cop, even though a retired one. I'll be at your home around seven as planned, and I want a big juicy sirloin steak."

168

"You got it boss, see you then." We finished and I hung up. It was good to have our favorite mischief maker back in the family.

**

Chapter 22

One really nice thing about Las Vegas is that they have every kind of store in the world for whatever you needed. If you're looking for authentic Chinese lanterns, they have a small Chinatown of stores, or if you need a wide variety of meats, they have stores for just meats. You can get any kind of reptile or animal from snakes to tigers in this town if you knew where to look. But right now I needed steaks, so I drove to my favorite butcher shop and went in to get about a million dollars worth of steaks. I wish I could take this place home with me. I knew that there are starving people in places like India, but they weren't getting my steaks. But then again they don't eat meat in India do they? I'm not a vegetarian, and I respect people for not putting things like meat in their bodies, but it left all the more for me.

I took my packages to the car, went to a party store next door and got plenty of refreshments and snacks for everyone, putting them in the car and then headed to the house. While driving I relaxed thinking of what Mason had told me about Reverend Ben. Could Ben be smoking us about his involvement in this case, could he be a killer? Was he stirring up the media with the killings to back up his vendetta against gambling, to get some press?

I remembered reading about a police case in California where two little old ladies got homeless people life insurance policies then murdered them, making it look accidental. They were called the Black Widow murderers. Sounded like what Ben was supposedly doing. And what about Stacey? Was Stacey just a loose woman who wanted sex like I wanted steak, or is she a real Black Widow. My first rule of being a private investigator was to pay attention to details, followed by suspecting everyone, especially good looking blondes, or redheads, or brunettes. Well, I get it.

My cell phone rang as I sat at a light just off the main road to our home, it was Penny. "Yes, dear?" I said as the light changed and I turned the car onto our road.

"Where are you? I've got crazy people here with balloons and people diving into my pool and you're out with the food somewhere." I was just coming up to the house and said I'd be there shortly. I told her about Mason coming too; she said that was good, he needed a few friends. I parked and was getting out of the car when Deacon breezed out of the house.

"You have the grilling stuff?"

I tossed the bag to him and said, "Here, you take charge of the burning of the carcasses. Oh, and I invited Don Mason, turns out he was an old buddy of Will's from years ago."

"Mason? He still mourning the loss of his girlfriend?"

"Yeah, I think it's eating at him. But he seems to be holding up, he says he quit drinking and gambling as a tribute to her, I hope he can keep it up. It's only been a couple months since she was murdered. But he has some interesting facts about RevBen to tell us. So he'll be here too."

"I know he's been ostracized by the other cops in his old precinct, they don't like it when a cop goes to the dark side. He's not a bad person, just did a stupid thing."

We went into the house and Deacon went straight through to the incinerator to start the fire. It was now just before seven and I was walking through a living room full of balloons, it was almost funny. Willy was having fits about the balloons and someone, I presume Penny, tied one to his collar so he was trying to get away from it.

I came out to the ugly statue of the Greek god pouring water from a pitcher into the Koi pond. I grabbed a handful of fish pellets and threw them to the huge goldfish that devoured them in short time. I came out to the pool and found Buck, Maria, Lynn and Lacey relaxing on air floats in the pool. Mac was sitting on a plastic chair by the side of the pool smiling at me, "Not a swimmer?" I asked. "Nope, I'm not a fan of it," he replied. "Welcome to the club," I said and sat next to him.

Deacon was at the incinerator having fun getting the steaks ready for grilling. Penny was standing by giving him instructions, which I thought was funny, since she wasn't much a cook. But she tried, bless her.

We all sat or stood around when we heard a voice, "Can anyone join this orgy?" I turned to see Trapper standing just past the statue holding on to about ten balloons in one hand and holding Willy in the other. I stood and went to him, taking Willy away and shaking his free hand. "Welcome, my good friend, to our home."

He smiled and got a big kiss from Penny and a bear hug from Deacon. He told the wet people to stay back; he'd get to them later. Then he went to sit on a plastic chair as he let one balloon go at a time, floating up in the air towards the mountains behind our home. It was funny watching him letting them go, like a big kid at his birthday party. "Whose idea was it for the balloons?" he asked.

"Blame Deacon and Lynn for that." I replied.

He looked to Deacon and said, "You remembered the time I filled the Captain's office with balloons on his birthday, didn't you?"

Deacon smiled and said, "Guilty."

I introduced Trapper to Mac and Lacey explaining their story. He smiled and said he was pleased to work with them now.

I turned to see Mason come through the side gate and he saw Will sitting with his back to him, so he held his finger to his mouth for silence. He sneaked up behind Trapper and flicked his ear. Trapper came up out of the chair ready to beat on someone. His eyes went wide when he saw Mason. "Damn, you old mother lover you. How the hell are you?" he said as he grabbed on to Mason with a big hug. They danced around a bit then separated.

"Great to see you again Will. I hear you're back in town now?"

"Yep, I'm back home, far from the damn snow and humidity of Michigan. I've heard you've had a rough time?"

"Yeah, but we can talk about that later, enjoy your party, we'll have plenty of time to reminisce." They came back to us and I told everyone to sit and relax while Deacon and I burned the meat. I went to the barbecue to see how Deacon was doing, he had everything under control. I picked out a beer from the cooler on the picnic table and watched everyone surrounding Trapper while he told them of his couple days back in Vegas.

Later after we ate our bounty and relaxed around the pool, Trapper pulled me aside. "I heard about your spider case, you need some help?"

"Boy, nothing gets by you," I laughed.

"Hey, I got ears all over this town, and the amazing thing is that I have been away for almost twenty-five years and yet it's no different. Well, the town has changed, but the people are the same. That's comforting."

"Glad to hear it. As for the spider killings, I'll fill you in on what I know later. Tonight we just celebrate your return." I patted him on the back and we went to the others all sitting by the pool relaxing.

About an hour later, I got Lynn and Mason together to talk about Reverend Ben and she and Deacon sat listening to him tell the tale. Buck and Maria said their good-byes; they both had to get up early for work, which I knew was an excuse. Maria worked nights and Buck, well, Buck set his own hours. Mac said he was going back home with Lacey to enjoy an evening with her before he went back to guarding Freddie in the morning, they left. I knew what they were going to do.

Trapper came up beside me as I stood watching the sun slip down the mountain behind us and we stood quietly for a moment. I finally said, "It's really good that you're here, I hated to leave everyone back in Michigan, but we needed the change. How do you feel about coming back to your roots?"

"Good, my mother is still back in Michigan, but I can go visit her, like you will with your family. Maybe I'll talk her into moving back, she grew up here too. If her husband would retire maybe they will. Okay, so do I get an office in your firm?"

I smiled and looked to him. "I got a small storeroom in the back of the building you can put a desk in. Did you get your P.I. license taken care of yet?"

"Yep, I got it pushed through, just have to get the permanent one from the Attorney General's office, but with the temporary one, I'm good to go."

"I'll get you the address of my building and we'll get you set up. It'll be strange working with you on an even footing. No longer a cop and a P.I., now two P.I.'s in a pod."

"That's peas in a pod," he laughed, "I get what you're saying. It will be like old times."

Penny came up on my other side and asked, "Are you two worshiping the sun gods?"

I smiled and said, "We're plotting the take over of Las Vegas. I'm going to be king."

"So that makes me the queen? I'll need a bigger house for all my servants."

"You got it.

**

Chapter 23

I sat in my office the next morning having arrived earlier than usual. Buck beat me in, I guess he liked being the boss and working on his schedules for his guards. We talked briefly about Trapper being back and that I was letting him join our team, Buck liked that. We cleaned the back room for Trapper's office and waited.

Later Buck was back in his office as I stopped at his door. He spoke, "Back when I was young and foolish and a drunk, Trapper was fair with me when I would get caught for driving like a madman. I do respect the guy for that and for all we've been through the last two years while playing detectives." He gave me his grin and sat back.

I heard the door open by the tinkle of the little

bell and looked out of Buck's office to see Trapper surveying the lobby. I went out to greet him, Buck came just after me.

"Well, ready to start the job?" I asked.

He stood still, looking at the front and said, "I guess I won't mind working out of here. Good neighborhood, good parking, nice view of the strip, centrally located, I like it so far. Now where is the storeroom you're going to let me use?" he smiled.

"Come on and I'll give you the tour." I took him and Buck around the place and then took him to the room that Buck and I cleaned out to let Trapper set up in. "I have a desk, chair and file cabinets ordered and will be in later today by delivery. You can decorate it anyway you want, just don't bring in any hookers." Trapper let out a loud laugh and gave me a hug. I was getting used to his hugs now so it didn't bother me; he was just an open kind of guy.

We sat on the couches in the lobby and talked. "Now tell me about your spider case," Trapper asked. I told him everything that I knew about the case and what we were doing about it. He smiled and said he'd like to help.

I said, "Good because I have something to do today that I would need help with, sort of a backup in a possible volatile situation."

Black Widow Murders

"Oh good, danger on my first day, thanks," he grinned.

I looked to Buck and said, "I may need a couple of your biggest armed guards to go with us, can you get them in soon?" he said he'd call two ball busters he had and have then in within the hour. He got up and went to his office to make his calls.

As we sat waiting for Buck to come back, I saw a furniture truck pull up to the front door. We got up and went to open the door for them as they brought in the office equipment. I showed them where to put the things and they unpacked them and set them up. They took the boxes back out to the truck and drove off. I went back to Trapper's new office and he was sitting at the desk with a big smile.

"This is so much better than that dingy office I had back in Clinton Township PD. I am going to like this."

Buck came in a said, "I got the men coming in, give them about a half hour. Do I pay them or you pay?" he asked with a grin.

"The company will take care of them, cheapskate. Besides the funds are all in one account so it's the company funds, not mine or yours. That's for tax purposes, not being greedy." I grinned back at him.

Trapper smiled and asked, "Do I get a pay check now or a cut of the client fees?"

"Uh, we'll discuss that later. Just be happy you have a job in this economy. Okay enough money talk; let's go back out so I can outline my plan of attack today on a few bookies."

"Bookies? I know a few, ones I rousted years ago. But they probably are all out of business now." Trapper said and stood. We went out to the lobby just as Buck's men came in through the back door. He signaled them to come up front and I was a bit surprised by their size, they were huge. Even Trapper had a look on his face. Buck introduced Carmine and Vinnie, a couple good Italian boys I presumed.

"Gentlemen, welcome, I have a mission to go on today, and I'll need you for protection from the criminal element. This person is Will Trapper, former homicide detective from back in Michigan, now a new partner of our firm. Let's have a seat and I'll tell you what I need." We sat on the couches and I started to talk.

"Okay, I have to go out and question a few bookies about who they may have taken book for in the WSOP tournament. I've been told by my source that these men don't like to talk about their clients, so I'll just have to sweet talk them. But if they get nasty, expect anything from them, is that agreeable?"

Black Widow Murders

Everyone nodded or grunted, I was satisfied. I asked Buck if he wanted to join us, but he had a new client coming in today to talk about guarding his business. I looked to Trapper and said, "Shall we roll?"

The four of us went out to my Crown Vic and the two beefy men got in back, barely. I looked at the first name on the list and started the car. "Ever hear of Benny Lewis?" I asked Will.

"Sweet Benny? Yeah, he's an institution around here, the cops even like him, he's old as the mountains around us, so he doesn't get busted too often. I've been in on a few of his busts when he was younger. He kept under the radar so we may not have too many problems if we are polite and don't threaten him," Trapper said.

"What kind of muscle does he have?"

"Well as I remember he had some knee busters in his employ, but they'd have to be old men by now, unless he's recruited."

"How does he work his business?"

"He's got a record store and has a room in the back that can disappear in a heartbeat, from what I remember."

We got to his record store and Trapper laughed

to see the improvements, "Business must be good." We parked and went to the building. There were huge posters of all the latest singers and bands across the front of the store and signs proclaiming all the sales going on. We went in and the place was busy with mostly teenagers floating around the racks of CD's and a few racks of vinyl records, mostly for collectors I presumed.

We went up to the sales desk and there was a strange looking girl standing with her mouth open when she saw our knee busters. "Hi, is Benny in?" I asked nicely. She took her eyes off the guys and looked to me, her eyes were black with heavy mascara, I could barely tell where her eyelids were.

"Benny is busy, do you have an appointment?" she squeaked.

"No just tell him we need some information, please." I asked even nicer now.

"Oh I can't bother him, he's in conference."

Trapper went over to a rack of CD's and pushed it over crashing it to the ground. "Gee, I'm sorry, can you get the owner so I can apologize," he said. She didn't move so Trapper walked to another rack and started to push when her eyes went wide and she yelled to wait.

She went off to a door at the back of the showroom and went in. Trapper smiled and said,

Black Widow Murders

"As a cop I probably would have gotten reprimanded for that, it felt good."

About two minutes later the girl came back out and said, "Mr. Lewis will see you now." She pointed to the door and we went to it. I said to Carmine to cover the door just in case. He smiled as I opened the door and Carmine stood with it open. Trapper, Vinnie and I went into the smallish room and found a wizen old man sitting behind a big oak desk with three LCD computer monitors almost hiding him. "You aren't the cops; I hope you aren't a rival store trying to muscle in on my record business, because I wouldn't like that." He was almost cute for an old fart.

"No Mr. Lewis, we're not here to give you trouble, I just have a couple questions then we'll leave you alone to your record business." I came around the side of his desk and I couldn't believe it, he was playing solitaire on his computer. "I'm a private investigator," pointing to Trapper," and this is my business associate and these other men do my leg work for me." I smiled at him.

"They probably could break legs," he said eyeing the big men. "What do you want?"

I sat on a chair next to his desk. "I just need to know who may have placed any real big bets on the finals of the WSOP. Mostly a player in the tourney who may have done it."

"Bets, I don't know from bets, what are you talking about? I sell records."

Trapper stepped forward and said, "Sweet Benny, don't lie to us, I used to haul your ass in back in the day for illegal book making."

Benny looked hard at Trapper, then his eyes squinted and he smiled. "Yeah, I can see it, you're Mike Trapper's boy, it's Will right?"

**

Chapter 24

Trapper was taken back when he heard his father's name. His dad was a cop in Vegas for years until he was shot in a gang related raid. "Yeah, but Dad is now deceased, murdered in a bad raid. You knew my dad?"

"He was a good cop, kind to me, used to come in once in a while to see if I was keeping out of trouble. He used to get a bang out of hearing his kid had arrested me. For you I'll give information. Now talk to me."

I said, "We just need to find out if one of the players in the WSOP finals was betting big time, and who that might be."

Black Widow Murders

"This have to do with the murders of those players?"

"Yes, we're trying to find out who may have murdered them. Can you help us?"

"I'm not saying I participate in anything illegal, but if I were a person who may have taken bets, I'd say none of the players might have placed a bet with me, if I were taking book."

I smiled and pulled out my list that Mason had given me. I set it in front of him and asked, "Do any of these fine gentlemen look like they may know something?"

He put on those half glass for reading and studied the list, smiling occasionally and then took his glasses off placing them carefully aside. He looked up to me, his eye were sunken and he had shopping bags growing under them, and said, "Two of these guys would take those bets, large ones, the kind murders are committed over. Number two and four are my suggestion if you want to save time running all over Vegas."

"You've been a gentleman, sir. Sorry to mess up your showroom." Trapper offered.

"Hell, that idiot girl out there needs the work; she thinks Sinatra is a rock group, dumb as a plank but works cheap."

I stood and said, "Thank you Mr. Lewis, appreciate your help."

We started to leave when the old man called Will; he turned as the rest of us went out. "Your dad was a good man, he was fair and kind for a cop, you should always be like him."

"I will sir, and I'll stop in every now and then to see if you're keeping out of trouble." Trapper smiled.

"You do that, I have things to tell you about him."

Trapper was the last to leave the room, he came out grinning. "What did he say?" I asked.

"He's going to enlighten me about my father. I have always had a fondness for hookers and shady characters like Sweet Benny; they have an ethic to their lifestyle that honest people could only hope to attain." He smiled and walked to the exit.

We drove over to the address of number two on the list. This place wasn't as nice as Benny's record shop; it was a rundown store selling second hand furniture and junk.

I parked around the side and the four of us gathered at the front and went in. Behind a counter was a woman who looked like she had been used a little too much. She must have been a good looker in her youth, but now the garish makeup and the scraggly hair made her look frightening. She nodded to me as I approached and asked if she could help us. She was watching Carmine and Vinnie carefully, probably wondering if we were mob related.

"I'd like to see Hector Reams, I was told by one of his associates that he might help me."

"And you are?" she wheezed through a haze of smoke from her self-rolled cigarette; it had no illegal odor so I presumed it to be tobacco.

"I'm Jim Richards, this is Will Trapper and the two big guys are Cheech and Chong. Is Hector in?"

She eyeballed me up and down then reached under the counter, I was ready in case she pulled a weapon, but she pushed a buzzer. I could hear it in the back.

She sat back and folded her arms, "hang on," was all she said.

After a minute's wait, a very big Samoan looking man entered through the bead curtain. He made my men look puny, but I'm sure my 9mm Glock could take care of him. He came to me and asked what I wanted.

"Are you Hector?" I asked.

"Hector's busy, what do you want?" he asked again.

"I need some information, do you give information?"

He looked to Trapper and my guys and made a face, like he was not amused by us.

I gave in and said, "I'm a private investigator, these men are my associates, I'm investigating two murders of the WSOP poker players and need to know if any of the players put any big bets down on the outcome. Can I see Hector now?"

"I'm Hector, who sent you?"

"Sweet Bennie, he thought you might be able to help us." He didn't say a word; he just turned and went back to the curtain. He looked back and motioned us to follow. I told Carmine to wait out here and cover our backs, he agreed. We went to the curtain and into a hallway where I saw Hector standing by a door waiting for us. He went in and we followed.

We found him about to sit at a desk, there were two younger men standing nearby looking like they could use a bath and a good haircut. I didn't find them threatening, they looked like light-weight gofers. Hector told them to wait outside and they went through another door behind him. It opened to the outside from what I could see, there was a couple cars parked back there.

Hector clasped his fingers together and looked like he was praying. He look at me over his hands and said, "You want to know about the murders of the poker players, I have nothing to tell. No one has placed any outstanding bets on the remaining players, although the deaths have changed the odds on all concerned. It puts me in a bad situation when an underdog suddenly moves up in the standings. My profit margin kind of sucks. It's like if a prize race horse dies at the starting line, all bets are suddenly at risk. The house can get screwed. I'd like these killings to stop, but I can't help. You have to remember that if your player is betting, they wouldn't do it themselves; they'd hire a beard to place the bet for them. I haven't had any big bets on the tourney, mostly small ones, nothing to signal a cause for murder."

I had thought about the possibility of the player having someone else place the bet, but there would be a huge amount placed which would send up my radar. "So there's nothing you know that could put me on the killer?"

"As I said, I have nothing for you. I hope you find the killer before he messes up the finals. That's all I have gentlemen, now I have work to do."

I thanked him and we went back out to the store. Carmine followed us out and to the car. He grinned and said they had a lot of good junk in there, he may come back to do some shopping. I laughed remembering years ago when I had a friend in the second hand business; one man's junk is another man's treasure they always say. I wondered just who "they" are, and how do "they" always know.

We drove to the number four listing that Sweet Benny recommended and it was a beauty salon. I was a bit surprised and Trapper was delighted. I parked on the side and told Carmine to wait out front of the building. The rest of us went in and it was like any other hair salon, but a bit nicer. The smell was overpowering, ammonia and hair bleach, creams and shampoos. I never like the smell, but put up with it. There was a girl at a small counter who looked like a cashier, I went to her and asked her if Sam was in. She smiled and asked what it was about.

"We were sent by Benny Lewis about a matter of importance. Is Sam in?"

The woman smiled and picked up her phone and pushed a button. She spoke into the old fashion handset and announced our request. She said a few more things about hair appointments and then hung up. She pointed to a door at the back of the room and said to go there.

We went to the door and it wouldn't open, I looked back to her as she pushed a button on the counter. I could hear the buzzing of a door lock opener and the door was released. We went through, finding ourselves in a larger room with many women sitting at tables and computer monitors. Trapper whispered, "This takes the place of betting slips now days. It's the electronic age taking over."

A very attractive redheaded woman came up to us, I could almost hear Trapper drool, he loved redheads. She said, "Greetings gentlemen, how's Benny doing nowadays?"

I smiled and said, "He's still alive. May I speak with Sam?"

"You're talking to her; didn't Benny tell you I was female?"

"Well, no he didn't. I guess he wanted it to be a surprise. And a pleasant surprise it is."

"Well, thank you Mr. Richards." She said making me wonder how she knew my name before I even told her.

She must have caught my surprised look and said, "I've seen you on TV about the crimes you have solved here in Sin City. I happen to be a big fan of police detectives and P.I.'s."

Trapper moved up front and said, "Surprising for the business you are in."

She gave him a big smile and said, "I can tell you're a cop, you have the look. Are you with Metro?"

"No, I'm from out of the Detroit area, but just recently retired back to my hometown of Vegas. Jim and I are working together; I'm a licensed P.I. now." Trapper was spreading his charms all over the woman. She looked to be in her fifties and attractive. I thought Trapper was going to ooze all over her.

"Intriguing. I figured you weren't here to bust me, since Benny sent you, now what can I do for you?"

I spoke, "I'm sure you are aware of the murders in the WSOP, we're investigating their deaths. I'm checking around to see if there have been any big bets placed on the players since the murders started."

"As a matter of fact we did get a very substantial bet on the one lesser player, you think maybe it's important?"

**

Chapter 25

Trapper moved closer, "Well, Sam... may I call you Sam?"

She gave him a big smile and said he could. He continued, "Please call me Will then. Now Sam, if you could bend your professional ethics just a little to allow us some info, we are trying to stop a murderer before he kills again. I hope we can work together on this to bring him to justice."

Trapper was giving her the whole cop bit figuring it may turn her on, the old dog. She was soaking it in.

"Well Will, I'm always interested in criminals being brought to justice, of course I mean murderers not little criminals like bookies. What do you need to know exactly?"

I spoke now over Trapper's shoulder, "We would need a name of the person who placed the bet."

"I don't like giving out the names of my clients, but if this helps, you just didn't get it from me, understand?"

"We'll handle it with the utmost care," Trapper said.

I was trying not to laugh, the poor guy was so obvious, it was funny. Sam went to a computer at a much larger desk, probably hers, and typed a few lines and then hit a button and out popped a paper from her laser printer. Ah, modern technology. She gave Trapper a big smile and the paper. He handed it to me and took her hand and asked if she was free some night for dinner. She looked surprised and said yes much too quickly. I just shook my head and thanked her for her kindness and help and said we'd be going so she could go back to her business.

Trapper actually gave her a kiss on the hand and smiled, then we went out. "Smooth move slick. You really had her in the palm of your hand," I said as we went back to the car.

"I'm in love. She's a goddess. I have to stop back here to arrange for our date soon."

We sat in the car and I looked at the betting slip and it had a bunch of code numbers and figures, the name was either made up or someone else other than our killer. It said J. Higgs for the name and the bet was two hundred thousand on Harold Carlisle.

"This doesn't prove that Harold is the killer, just that someone likes him to win now, or it's

Harold and he thinks he can win. But if Freddie is still in the race, that would upset the standings. I think we need to watch Freddie a little closer."

I called Lynn and she said that Reverend Ben was missing now. They couldn't find him or Stacey anywhere. She had warrants out on both of them for obstruction of justice. I told Lynn about what we found and said we'd talk more about it later. She said she'd do a search on LEIN and NCIC on J. Higgs, if he was even a real person. I said I was going back to see Freddie and ask him a few more questions. Lynn said she'd let me know if they found either of our runaways and hung up.

I looked to Trapper and said, "I'm going to drop off our body guards, even if we didn't need them, and go to the Rio." I looked back to Carmine and Vinnie and thanked them. They said it was fun.

I drove up to the office and I stopped in to see if Penny was there.

Lacey smiled and said, "Penny decided to go shopping at the Boulevard Mall, she said she was going straight home afterwards." I thanked her and told Buck we were going to the Rio if anyone needed us.

"Did you have any problems?" he asked watching Carmine and Vinnie heading to the back door.

"I'm a little disappointed that we didn't have a little more action but Trapper got a date out of it."

"Speaking of that, can you run me off a few business cards on your computer so I can give them out to all the beautiful women I'm going to meet now." He grinned and handed me his old business card from Michigan, "Just use the same cell phone number, but add all the good stuff you have on your card."

"You're going to need to get a local number, this one is good for Michigan area code, it's a long distance number from here to call you," I said.

"Well, go ahead and make a couple till I can fix it."

I turned to Buck and said, "Okay, we'll be at the Rio talking to a few people. If Lynn or Deacon stop by tell them where we are." He said he'd take care of it and Trapper and I went back to my car. We drove out to the Rio and I called Mac to let him know we were coming.

I took Trapper up to the tenth floor and Mac opened the door for us. Freddie was back at the card table with his peeps; I came over and said I needed to talk to him privately. He put his cards down and stood. Freddie, Trapper and I went to the bedroom where I introduced Trapper to Freddie.

I told Freddie to sit, he sat on the bed as

Black Widow Murders

Trapper and I sat on the easy chairs. "I need to ask you about the bets placed on the players, how does it affect the game?"

"Well, we players don't pay much attention to the betting that goes on, sure we like to see people bet heavy on us, makes us feel good. We don't get any of the payouts, so we don't care. I'm shooting for the million dollar prize."

"Tell me about Harold Carlisle, what kind of person is he?"

"Harold? He's a good guy, a little stuck up and sometimes too over confident in his abilities as a card man, but he's okay."

"I need to ask you something that you need to keep to yourself, I mean it, this can't go out of this room."

"Yeah, sure, what is it?"

"What would you say if you knew there was a two hundred thousand dollar bet placed on Harold to finish?"

Freddie stared at me and then he made a face, "Someone has way too much faith in Harold or knows something we don't. He couldn't murder off all of us to win, he needs someone to play against or they'd call off the competition. He's not that good to beat me, or Sara. Mathew Langer is borderline; I

196

think he'll crash, so it's up to me, Harold and Sara. This is so wrong, Harold couldn't be the killer, he's always around someone in the tourney, we'd know if he went off to kill someone."

"Harold wouldn't have to do the kills himself, he could hire someone." I looked at the betting slip Sam gave me, "If Harold wins, someone is going to take home over a million dollars in payout."

"Does the WSOP know this, it's a big bet?"

"This was done off of the legal process, through a bookie. So there would be no suspicions about the crimes and the players."

"Now I'm wondering about Harold," he said.

"You have to keep this to yourself, we need to catch him or whoever is setting this up, and don't want to tip their hand that we know, it may blow the whole thing, understand."

He agreed.

My cell phone rang and it was Lynn, I excused myself and went over by the windows looking out over the city, "Yeah, I'm here."

"We found Reverend Ben; he's in LV medical, hanging on from spider bites." I was a bit shocked by what she said. "He was found wandering outside of his church by his street people, they called an

Black Widow Murders

EMS and he was taken to LV Medical where they have been keeping him alive. Luckily he didn't get bit by too many of the bastards, so he had time to get help. He can't talk right now but I have men at this church checking for the scene where he was attacked. Deacon was betting on Stacey as the culprit, but I'm not so sure now since about ten minutes ago we got a hit on one of her credit cards being used in Boulder City, she's too far away to have done it. I called Boulder City PD and asked them to track her down and I've got two men heading there to pick her up. This is getting complicated. We can rule out the both of them, we have a serial killer with a different agenda. I need to talk to you more about the betting thing you found out; it may be a new lead."

I said I'd come over to the precinct and we'd regroup. I hung up, took Trapper aside and told him what had happened.

"Freddie, we have to go, but remember what I said, mum's the word," I said and we left.

~~*~~

The man returned to his basement not happy that the reverend escaped death from his spiders. A hour and half ago he had hid in the church balcony waiting for Reverend Ben to enter, just after he made his way to the pulpit and put the special box he made full of spiders on the altar. He knew the reverend would see the box and open it. He wanted to watch as the spiders were sprung out of the box and latch on to the preacher. Unfortunately the box didn't quite work the way he planned and it only released a few spiders, but they were upset enough to bite. The reverend realized what had happened and was dousing himself with water from an urn of flowers off the altar to wash off the spiders. He ran to the front entrance and out to the street screaming for help. The man ran down the stairs from the balcony to retrieve his box and shook off the remaining spiders, taking the box out the back way. He sat in his basement mad that he hadn't killed the man who was defiling his love, his LadyLucky.

**

Chapter 26

We sat in Lynn's office brainstorming. I spoke, "I think we need to start back at the beginning. Harvey Trent is murdered, by black widow spiders and stamped on the head with a spider. He was one of the players in the WSOP tourney and married to Stacey, AKA LadyLucky. Stacey wants to hire me to keep her from being suspected, but she has an alibi, a mystery man who she said was one of the players, a lie. Freddie comes to me wanting protection after getting the spider card, why the card, a warning? Then I get a threatening call. Another warning? We talk to Freddie's friends and then catch the reporter. By the way, whatever happened to him?"

Lynn smiled, "We let him soak up the ambience of our cells with real criminals over night, he was very happy to be let out. Didn't like criminals after that. I suspect we'll be reading about his mistreatment, but it'll blow over."

"Okay, so he's a red herring, now we get an attempt on Freddie from the drink container and we figure it's because of his poker ties. But I find out about the Twitter connection with Stacey and the players. Kepler sets up a meeting with Stacey and he gets flushed, sorry, but I can't resist the image of him on the toilet, dead." Everyone gave a suppressed snicker and I continued. "Then we find Reverend Ben and his connection with Stacey, he's the real person who spent the night with her when her husband was being killed. We talk to him; he finds out that Stacey, his big love, hasn't been faithful. Then the biggest crime of this case happens, Trapper reappears." I laughed as I looked to him.

"Screw you Richards, you'll need me." He smirked.

I went on, "Okay, so I get an idea, I do that occasionally, I go talk to Mason who gives up a few bookies and Trapper and I go visit a few of them, finally finding that there is a huge bet on Langer to win. Now I find out that Reverend Ben has been hit by the Spiderman. He's not in the tourney so why?"

"He was a lover of Stacey, AKA LadyLucky," Deacon added.

"Right! All the murders or attempts were against men who associated or spent the night with Stacey. She's our link to the killings." I sat back waiting to see what reaction I'd get.

"Someone is in love with her and doesn't like the players only because she is flirting with them," Trapper spoke now.

I held my finger to my nose and pointed to him, "Bingo!"

"But how do we find out who he is?" Lynn asked.

"I thought about that, he seems to be wanting to kill off these men he feels threatened by, so let's set up a meeting with a new love for LadyLucky and set a trap," I said.

"That I like," Lynn said. "How are you going to work it?"

"The best means of communication we have, Twitter," I smiled. "I'll get back on as LadyLucky and have someone give me the whole sex spiel and we'll set a place and time, then wait him out."

"Let's do it, you can use my computer," Lynn said.

I moved over to her computer and did some magic on the keys and got Twitter up and running. "I just set up a fake account for myself as PokerChips and I have Stacey's account in a different window, that way I can do the talking for both. I hope this guy is watching or else he checks her timeline." I had both accounts up and started to talk to myself. Lynn was watching over my shoulder as I typed hot and heavy sex talk.

Lynn laughed and said, "You should try writing romance novels instead of crime."

"What's wrong with my crime novels?" I asked.

"Nothing, but you sure can dirty talk up a good one."

"Well, I'm spreading it on a little thick, but we have to be sure he's real mad about this."

I finished the chat and clicked off the line. I sat back and said, "I have the two of them meeting at the Wayfarer Motel tonight at nine, but I said I would be there at seven to get the room ready for our tryst. That may bring the killer out figuring he'll take care of business before Stacey gets there.

I hope this works."

"So do I," Lynn said.

~~*~~

The man was really fuming now as he brought up LadyLucky's profile that showed what she had said in the last couple hours. He saw the talk between someone called PokerChips and his love. This was getting intolerable, all these men chasing after her, and he knew she was weak, so he forgave her for meeting with them. He decided that he wouldn't fail with this one, so he went to get his suit and gather extra spiders this time. After a while he had the container filled with his beasts and plotted out his attack. He got the real name for the PokerChips screen name and found out he was called Walt Whitman. He called the Wayfarer and said he was confirming his reservation for a room tonight under Walt Whitman. The clerk said they had the reservations and then the man asked what room he was going to be in, the woman said room five. He thanked her and hung up. Stupid woman shouldn't be giving out room numbers, but it was a cheap motel so they don't stand on protocol. He would be ready now.

~~*~~

Black Widow Murders

I said, "The killer has seen me and just about everyone else on this case so we need to send in someone he hasn't seen." I looked to Trapper.

"Oh sure, you want me to go in and be eaten by spiders," he grinned.

"They don't eat you they bite, and we will be all around the place to protect you. Besides, I don't think a spider could even bite through your tough old hide."

He gave me a middle finger up the side of his head and said, "I'll do it but I get combat pay."

"Take it up with our accountant," I said.

Trapper got a glow in his eyes and said, "Hey I just realized, I can't pull my badge and yell 'freeze, police' anymore. What do I do now, show my license and yell 'P.I.'?"

"I usually just pull my Glock and yell, go ahead make my day," I said.

Lynn was laughing and said for us to just behave. We left to go set up our plan for catching the killer. It was now almost five o'clock and we drove up to the Wayfarer and got the room paid for. We went in and checked it for places to hide and ways to get in and out. The bathroom had the only window in the place other than the front window.

Bob Moats

The bathroom window was big enough for someone to slip into; Lynn reached over the toilet and unlatched the window. "Just making it easier for the killer to get in," she said.

She told Warren and another one of her men to sit tight in the room and they could hide in the closet if someone comes in before the time Trapper would arrive. Warren clicked on the TV and sat back, Lynn said not to get too comfortable. He smiled at her and said he'd stay awake. I brought in four spray cans of the spider killer and put them around the room, telling Warren and his partner how to use them. They examined the cans and said they would be fast on the draw if needed.

Lynn said, "There's not much we can do here for now and it would better if we weren't all hanging around in case he comes early, so let's go get something to eat. Warren keep your cell phone handy, I'll call you as we gather outside."

~~*~~

The man had made up the balsa wood box and put it in a plastic grocery bag, then in a larger cardboard box to protect it on the way to the motel. He was going to go to the room just after eight and smash it in the face of the damn pervert who waited for his woman. The balsa wood was fragile enough to bust open so he brought gloves to protect his hands from the spiders and to leave no fingerprints. He had his sunglasses and ball cap ready to wear. He went up to his car parked behind the building and drove out to get something to eat before he made his kill.

~~*~~

We had eaten our dinner and I called Penny to tell her what we were up to. She said, "That's nice, I'm busy trying on the new clothes I bought today to wear for the show, oh and I bought you a couple new shirts, yours are getting a little worn." I cringed. Penny had great taste in women's clothing but she had bought me clothing in the past and I tried to not wear her selections too often. I didn't like pastel colors.

"That's nice dear, I'll be home as soon as we catch us a killer, shall I bring him home to try on my shirts?"

"If you'd like, that would be punishment enough. I'll see you later."

I wondered why she said the shirts would be punishment, then I started to really worry. I hope she hadn't bought any Hawaiian shirts for me. I turned to Trapper and asked if he was ready.

"As I'll ever be," he replied.

It was now six-thirty and Lynn said it was time to set up the sting. We were going to have Trapper go in the office and pretend he was registering and then go to the room and wait. I hoped the man would come to the door with some excuse and try something.

We arrived at the motel and Trapper was using Warren's car since the killer knew my car, which I left across the street so it would be out of sight. There were two other unmarked cars waiting far enough away so to not be seen. I sat in Lynn's unmarked car down from the room as Trapper pulled up to it and got out. We got a grocery bag of drinks for him to take in, trying to look as normal as possible. He went to the office and came out a few minutes later and went to the room, using the key to get in. Lynn had called her men inside and said he was coming so they were ready. Trapper went in as we sat waiting.

About ten minutes later, just around eight-fifteen a man came walking around the building, he had on a hat and sunglasses and was carrying a plastic grocery bag. He came to Trapper's door and stopped. He looked around and then knocked, Lynn called on her radio, "He's here, let's go!"

**

Chapter 27

Everyone started to head for him as Trapper opened the door with his revolver pointed at the killer. He had already taken the balsa box out of the bag and when he saw the gun, he panicked and crushed the box tossing it at Trapper. Will saw pieces of wood and tiny black dots coming at him and fell back into the room as the man turned to run back down the side of the building, back to where he came from.

We had been just a bit too far away to get to him in time as he ran around the back. Lynn, Deacon and two other detectives came running up to the side and Lynn yelled for one of the detectives to go back to his car and watch the road in case he had a car. Lynn came up to a fence that the man must have jumped over as she was scanning the parking lot of the party store next to the motel when she saw a dark maroon GTO driving out of the lot at a high rate of speed. She called on her radio to the waiting car and gave the description and said to keep him in sight. Lynn and Deacon headed back to her car as I said I was going to check on Will, I'd follow later. They got to their car and drove off following the direction given them.

I got to the room and went in cautiously finding Trapper standing without a shirt as Warren and Smith were spraying him and the floor with the bug killer. He looked to me and gave me a half smile. I went up and checked him for bites but saw none, I said he was lucky. He said he wanted a raise. I said I was going to follow Deacon and Lynn, they were on chase. Trapper said he was going to sit out this chase and take a shower. I agreed he needed one and left before he could hit me.

I got to my car across the road and called Deacon on my cell phone and asked where they were. He said they drove up the Boulevard then were going East on Bonanza. From there he wasn't sure where they were going. I came up to Bonanza and turned right, driving down a little ways till I saw them cruising around, watching for the car. I saw them stop and pull into a church parking lot, at least I thought it was a church, it was an old brick and stone building and it had a big cross on the front. I pulled up beside them and got out; Deacon yelled that they saw the GTO parked on the side of the building.

I came up and Lynn said this was Reverend Ben's church. That took me by surprise, what did Ben have to do with the spider killer. We all went into the building and Lynn said to split up. I had my Glock out and checked the coat rooms up front, Deacon said he was going to check the second floor lofts and Lynn spotted a door next to the altar, saying she was going that way.

Lynn went into the door and found it was a

very narrow stairway going down. The stairs were wide enough for only one person to go up or down, she went down. She came out into what looked like a recreation room, it had tables and chairs and a ping-pong table. She surveyed the room and saw no one. She walked around the room watching every corner for the killer. She saw a short hallway that ended at an open door, she went to it.

It was dark in the room behind the door, she reached for a light switch but when she flipped it, nothing happened. She pushed the door open checking the crack to see if someone was behind the door. There were only two small basement windows that let in a little light but the room was still dark enough to hide someone. She cautiously entered and saw the overhead light bulb was broken, and she felt this was a sign that the killer was nearby. She held her gun up wishing she had her flashlight. She saw a few chairs and a table with an old looking computer on it; she saw a coat rack with some clothing hanging and a box to the side that had stenciled "Lost and Found" on it. She moved in further and saw another door that was opened all the way but the room was dark. She went to the room and stood just at the threshold not wanting to go any further into the pitch black. She saw hanging on a hook next to the door a strange rubber suit, wondering what it was for.

Suddenly she felt hands on her back and she was pushed into the room and the door was slammed shut behind her. As she was falling into the room she put her hands out to break her fall and when she hit ground her wrist twisted and forced her to lose her gun in the dark room. She lay on the ground not moving, just listening. She was too frightened too feel around for the missing gun but she had to do something. She took out the cigarette lighter she carried even though she didn't smoke and spun the tiny wheel. The lighter caught and she froze in terror as she saw the cotton candy webs over her and the tiny dots lacing the webs with spiders.

She could feel her heart pounding and her neck and face broke out in a cold sweat. The flame on the lighter was going down, she knew it was old and she was now afraid it would empty out. She looked to her right and saw a foot high pile of newspapers and grabbed the top issue. She quickly rolled it and held the flame to the end of the roll. Unfortunately the paper was very old and dry; it started to flame up higher and hotter than Lynn had planned. It started to burn down fast and it singed her hand, causing her to drop the flaming paper. It was close enough to the pile that the rest started to flame up. She now had enough light to see the thousands of spiders now also panicking because of the flames, her heart about burst, pounding so hard, she started to beat on the door and screaming at the top of her lungs.

Deacon and I met in the main part of the church by the altar and I said I smelled smoke. We saw the door that Lynn had gone in and went to it,

211

going down. The smell was getting harsher now and I saw a door that had wisps of white floating out. We ran to it and saw the closed door with smoke coming out from cracks. We stood as we heard a small pounding and Deacon ran to the door but there was a lock on it. Deacon brought up his service revolver and fired on the lock blowing it off. He yanked on the door and smoke billowed out causing us to get low to the ground as the smoke rose up. Deacon's heart skipped a beat as he saw a hand and arm on the ground just in the doorway. He reached out and pulled hard, I started to grab on and pulled also.

We pulled Lynn out and away from the now burning room. I could see in the light of the flames all the spiders and their webs going up in the fire. I turned to see a large CO_2 fire extinguisher in the other room and ran to get it. Deacon was trying to bring Lynn around and she started to cough loudly from the smoke in her lungs. I was spraying the room and the flames were dying in the CO_2 spray from the extinguisher. Deacon lifted Lynn and took her to the other room and put her on a table. I came out after being sure the fire was out.

Two of the other detectives came running down the stairs from the front of the building and Deacon yelled to keep searching the building and around it, the killer had to be nearby. They went off as Lynn was now sitting up and when she saw Deacon she grabbed on to him with a hug I thought would strangle him.

We heard gun fire from above and Lynn said she was good to go. We went up the front stairs coming out to the front of the building and didn't see anyone. One detective came running in and said the killer got into his car and sped off. He called it in and put a BOLO out.

Lynn called the officers watching Reverend Ben at his hospital and asked if he was lucid enough to talk. The officer said he was awake now so Lynn hung up and said we were taking a trip to talk to the preacher and find out what the hell was going on.

I followed them in my car as we arrived at the hospital and went to Ben's room where we found him awake now but looking bad. Lynn went up and asked him point blank who the man was in his basement.

Ben look confused and asked, "What man?"

"The guy with the maroon GTO."

"Gregg? He's my handy man, bus driver and janitor. Why do you ask?"

"He was the man who tried to kill you with spiders, that's who he is and he's the man killing all the poker players. Talk to me Ben; tell me everything you know about him."

Chapter 28

"I can't believe that Gregg would try to kill me." Ben said in disbelief.

"Well, we almost burned down your church about thirty minutes ago trying to catch him. Did you know there was a room in your basement that harbored millions of Black Widow spiders?"

"No, I don't go into Gregg's room, was that where the spiders were kept?"

"Yep, and Gregg was killing poker players, not because he hated poker and gambling, but he hated men having affairs with Stacey, how's that for a downer?"

"I'm shocked. How did he know I was meeting with Stacey?"

"Twitter. He was on and saw every man chasing after her. Did you know he had an account?"

"Uh, I think he mentioned one time that he was on Twitter when I said I used it to protest gambling. But I wasn't paying much attention to him. I never did pay much attention to him, he was just the handyman."

"Does he live in the basement or does he have his own place?"

"I don't know that either. He comes and goes, he showed up one day last year looking for work and he had experience in maintenance so I hired him. He took that room in the basement to use as his workshop; I just stayed out of it."

"What's his full name?"

"Gregg Wakeman, he told me he grew up around here in Vegas. I really don't know much else about him."

I came to the side of his bed and said, "You know if you are going to build a religious empire, you need to keep better track of the people around you, especially your enemies."

Lynn pulled her cell phone and called in the name to get a read on his driver's license. She waited then pulled her note pad out and wrote down an address. Luckily he was the only Gregg Wakeman listed in Vegas. She said to Deacon that she had a place to go and they went out, I followed as fast as I could. I figured Lynn wanted to get Wakeman for pushing her into the spider's den. I almost felt sorry for him.

Black Widow Murders

We drove back up the Boulevard again to Charleston and then east to Boulder Highway. Just past Boulder we arrived to a small subdivision and Lynn waited for back-up since she had called on the way over. We parked down the road from his address, where we could see the tail of the GTO in the driveway between the houses. Because of the car she had probable cause to enter the house.

Three other cars came flying up and Lynn led the charge on the house. After a few minutes of searching the place they came up empty handed and Lynn was not happy. One officer came in saying he found tracks in the back yard leading out to an alley behind the house, they looked to be motorcycle tracks. He said he called for a BOLO but didn't know what kind of motorcycle to watch for, so they'd have to check them carefully.

Lynn was looking frustrated and said she was going back to the precinct and wait to see if anything would turn up. I looked at my watch and it was now almost nine-thirty and said I had it for the night. I called Trapper to see how he was doing, he said he was going to go home and take another shower; he still had a creepy feeling from the spiders. I said I'd see him in the morning at the office; he agreed and disconnected the call.

Everyone left Wakeman's house, but Lynn put a detail to watch the place in case he returned. I said I'd see them tomorrow and drove out to my home pulling into the drive, I could see the lights were on in the back so I figured Penny was swimming. I went through the house and out the patio door, stopping to feed the fish under the Greek god. I wondered how I got stuck with the job; I didn't even like the thing. Some night I might come out and push the damn statue over. I came around and saw Penny lounging on the chaise and came up as she looked to me with a smile.

"So did you catch your killer?" she asked.

"Got away, twice. But they're closer to knowing who he is now. They're watching for him, it's a matter of time now. Did you spend you're limit for clothes today?"

"Nope, I have a couple more trips to do before I have my entire summer wardrobe. Your new shirts are hanging in the bedroom; I like them so wear them more than once a month to please me."

It sounded a little like a threat, so I went in the house to look at them. I found the shirts and they actually looked good. One was all black with fire flames shooting up around the bottom hem. I had seen a man wearing this shirt one day and commented on it. Penny must have found it and bought it for me.

I put the shirts in the closet and came out to the kitchen. Penny was there throwing some TV dinners in the microwave. "Ah, gourmet cooking tonight?" I asked.

"Well, when you don't have the decency to call and let me know when you're going to be home, this is all you get." She kissed me on the nose and went off in the house somewhere leaving me to watch the food spin in the microwave. I yelled to her, "I like the shirts."

After we ate we watched TV and I was glad that there were no phone calls. We watched the last of our favorite late night talk shows so we crawled into bed. I was bushed but Penny was in a frisky mood, probably worked up from her shopping spree and I wasn't one to turn down a sexy woman like her. We wrestled for a while then cuddled. Penny was, of course, asleep quickly as I lay there doing too much thinking. I finally dozed off.

Morning came with a phone call; I knew it was too good to be true, that I could get through a morning without the evil call. Penny mumbled something about shutting off the alarm as I picked up my cell. "Hello," I spoke before looking at the caller ID.

It was Lynn, she said, "Freddie's in the hospital." My eyes came open and I sat up, "What happened?"

"Seems he heard that the spider killer had lost his weapons and Freddie felt like going out to celebrate. He asked Carlisle, Langer and Sara to go with him to a lounge to have one last fling before the finals today." I had forgotten about the finals. "Mac went with them to keep an eye on Freddie and when they finished up, everyone else left and Mac went to get the car as Freddie waited at the entrance to the lounge talking to a friend. As Mac was driving up he saw a car jump the curb and plowed into Freddie just missing his friend, then drove off fast. Mac and the people standing out front called for EMS, he's alive but broke up bad. Looks like the playing field just got narrower."

After seeing Penny off I went out to the Crown Vic and drove to Desert Springs Hospital to see Freddie and Mac. I had called Mac and told him I was coming, he said he'd fill me in when I got there. I parked and went in finding Mac in the waiting room, "How is he?"

"He's stable but still unconscious. Man I would never have left him alone if I thought this would happen, I figured since the spider guy was on the run and had no bugs to throw, Freddie would be safe but I still hung in. Then we were going to the car and a friend stopped him to talk about the finals and I said I'd get the car. I was driving up when this dark blue SUV came barreling from the side and plowed into Freddie. He flew up and hit the pavement hard. The SUV drove off, it was a deliberate attack."

I didn't think Wakeman would go after any of the players, so I was figuring it was the person who placed the big bet, getting rid of the best player of the four. "Where were Carlisle, Langer and Sara?"

"They had left about twenty minutes before we did, Freddie was still enjoying the music but I reminded him of the finals today. He said he was ready to go and this happened. Damn I feel bad."

"Don't let it get to you, you couldn't have known. You fulfilled your obligation to protect him from the spider killer; this is a whole new crime." I patted him on the back and said to hang in here and let me know if there are any changes. He looked so bad; I just let him be and said, "I'm going to the Rio for the finals, to see what is going to happen now." I left him and went to my car.

I called Lynn, "What's the word on Wakeman?"

"Nada, he's in the wind. Weber is not happy, but the case has been solved, we just need the killer. I sometimes wonder why people love so hard, enough to kill for it. Damn shame."

"Where are you now?" I asked.

"Deacon and I are at the Rio, waiting for the finals to start, if they start. No one has made a decision yet, so we'll see. Although there is going to be television coverage of the thing, I'm sure they will have some obligations to finish it even with less players. Are you coming over?"

"I'm on my way, be there shortly." I finished driving to the Rio and parked, going to the convention hall where I saw Warren standing by the entrance. He smiled and let me go through the gate where I would have had to pay, but he told the guy standing there I was with the police. I went in and found Lynn, Deacon and surprisingly, Trapper standing off the side of where the table was set up for the game. There were television cameras around the table and I saw Carlisle, Langer and Sara talking to someone who looked official. They were smiling and then went to sit at the table as the official pointed out their chairs.

The announcer came on the P.A. and did his spiel, then the color commentators at a table from off the side started talking to the cameras. The crowd was active and waiting for the games to start.

I was watching Harold Carlisle, the big bet of the day looking smug, did he have a secret?

**

Chapter 29

I was never really interested in poker, especially Texas Hold-em. Now Penny was the card shark, I wish I had her here to explain what was going on. We stood watching the cards being dealt and I could hear the commentators speaking in hushed tones for the home audiences. The game went on for a number of hands and then it was coming to an end for Langer, he played well but the cards were not in his favor. He stood and the crowd cheered him as he moved off. Sara and Carlisle were now playing against each other. I remember Freddie saying that Sara had a stronger chance to win, but it seemed like Carlisle was holding his own. The cards were dealt a number of times and it was pretty much evened up then Sara did something interesting, she put it all in. Carlisle sat back staring at her and then his cards, I could see his wheels turning. Was she bluffing or did she have what it would take to win.

Carlisle saw the raise and then put down his cards. Sara had a strange look on her face and went out. The crowd cheered loudly as Carlisle was proclaimed the winner. Sara stood and put her cards aside. She turned and went off into the crowd that was now moving towards Carlisle, I watched her until she was totally immersed in the crowd. I went over and while everyone was busy patting Carlisle on the back, I lifted Sara's cards. I knew just enough to know that she had a winning hand. I squared up her cards and put them in my pocket. I went to Trapper and asked him to come with me.

We went in the direction that Sara had gone and the only way out was a door off the side. I went to it, opened the door and Will and I went out into the heat and sunshine. I scanned the parking lot to see if I could spot Sara, but couldn't find her.

"Will, did you get Sam's number?" I asked.

"Yeah, whatcha need?"

"Call her and ask if we can stop by." That made him happy and he called her. I couldn't hear her side of the conversation but I figured it was good. "She says she's looking forward to our visit," he said. We went to my car and drove out to her beauty shop and parked on the side. Trapper was raring to go in; Sam was in the salon side waiting for us.

"I just got a call from my big bettor; they said they were coming to collect because they had a plane to catch out of town. I'm close to being tapped out making a one point two million dollar pay out."

"You may not have to cover that bet if my hunch is correct." I asked if we could wait in the back. Sam led us there and we waited. Trapper was pouring out his charms and gave her the new card I printed up for him last night.

"Are we still good for dinner?" he asked.

"You name the time and place and I'll be ready."

I was trying to ignore them so I wandered around the tables with women sitting at computers taking in betting slips from all over the place. Some gave me a suspicious look but most generally ignored me. After about ten minutes Sam's desk phone rang and she answered. She looked to us and nodded. Trapper followed me to stand behind the door coming into the room, as we heard the door buzzer sound. The door opened and in walked a young man and he approached Sam, but his back was to us. He handed her his copy of the betting slip for proof it was his bet. I whispered something to Trapper and he went out of the room. I came up behind the man and tapped him on the shoulder, he turned. When I saw his face I recognized him, he was one of Freddie's peeps who played poker with him in his hotel room and Freddie had called him Louie. He got a surprised look on his face; he must have remembered me from our questioning.

"Strange you being here Louie, did you have some inside info on the outcome of the finals? Could you have known that Carlisle was going to win? Or did you know that Sara was going to throw the game?" I pulled the cards from my pocket and fanned them in his face. He went blank as Sam said, "bets are invalid for fixed games, Sonny boy."

The door opened and Trapper entered dragging Sara by her arm. She was protesting but when she saw me she went quiet.

"Look who I found out in the lobby. Little Miss Loser."

I went to Sara, "So you figured that if you won the finals you'd come away with a million, of course you'd have to pay taxes, so it would be less. Now if you placed an illegal bet, there would be no taxes and you'd make even more than a million at the new odds because of the deaths of a few players." I held up the cards to her. "You decided to put in everything to lose, that would also take suspicion off you for Freddie getting mowed down. You'd be out of town with your booty and no one would be any the wiser. But you didn't count on us." I pulled two chairs over and told them to sit. I turned to Trapper, "You still have your handcuffs?"

He smiled and said, "It's hard to part with them." He pulled them out and handcuffed the two of them together as I pulled my cell phone.

Lynn answered after two rings and I said, "Lynn we worked out who Freddie's attacker was and a little fraud dealings on the WSOP. But I need some assurance to your discretion, we have a delicate situation involving Trapper's new girlfriend, she happens to be a bookie." I heard Lynn laugh and asked where we were. I said we would meet in the beauty salon for the pick up. I'd explain later.

After Lynn's men took the two young criminals out of the salon, Lynn smiled at Sam, "How are you doing Samantha, long time, no see?"

Black Widow Murders

"I'm good Lynn, now that I'm out of the business."

"And into a new one. I'm overlooking this just so we can close up this case, but if I get a complaint, well you know."

"I keep my clients happy, there'll be no complaints. Good to see you again." Sam smiled at Trapper as he stared at her. "I used to be an escort for a fancy club in town, so now you know my past."

Trapper grinned and said, "Oh, Baby, you have made me really happy." I laughed out loud making everyone look to me. I said, "It's a long story, I'm sure Trapper will share it with Sam."

Everyone was vacating the salon as I started to follow them, I turned to see Trapper still with Sam, I heard her say, "So do you always carry handcuffs?" That's when I went out, I didn't need to hear more. I sat in my car waiting for Trapper, who came strolling out a few minutes later.

"A former hooker, and beautiful, you are going to be unbearable now." He just smiled at me and we left.

We drove to Metro and in to see Lynn and Deacon. They were sitting in her office filling out papers, as Lynn looked up and said, "I don't like having to do reports any more than dealing with spiders, which are now all destroyed. I sent a team out to make sure the basement was sprayed and sanitized to be sure. Now we got every road and all the airports covered watching for Wakeman. We got his picture off his driver's license so they can identify him. If he tries to slip out we'll get him. Oh and thanks you two for catching Sara and her little friend. We'll get them to rat on each other."

"Well I guess you don't need my services anymore?" I asked.

"Not unless you got Wakeman in your pocket. Thanks again."

"Okay, we'll be going to see if we can stir up some real crimes." I smiled and we went out. At the car Trapper said his car was in the police lot and he was going back to see Sam. I shook my head and said to not get into trouble. He went off and I got in my car and drove to my office.

Lacey was working on some papers as I came in, she smiled and said, "I just talked to Mac, he said Freddie is going to be all right. He has some bruises and two broken bones but will survive. The TV has been covering the big win of Carlisle, how'd that work out?"

"All the crooks are in their cell tonight, we can sleep easy now. Sara figured if she could get Freddie out of the finals, it was going to be easier to control the win. Is Buck in?"

"No, he went out to a new client's car lot to set up his men; he said he'd probably hang there most the night."

I headed towards my office; I was tired for some reason. I sat in my chair as Willy came in and wanted up on my lap. I picked him up and gave him a noogie and put him on the client chair next to me. He did his little spin and plopped down watching me.

I was wondering where Penny was, it was after noon and she wasn't here. Then I remembered she was going to do some more shopping, oh well, it's her money.

**

Chapter 30

My cell phone rang, it was Lynn. "Just can't stay away from me can you?"

"Oh, I can try, believe me. I just called to say we got Stacey finally. They brought her in just after you left. I talked to her and she doesn't know a Gregg Wakeman, or so she says. I don't know what name he went by on Twitter, can you find out?"

I was already reaching for my computer and brought up the Twitter screen, "I'm checking now, if he used his real name to sign up, it will be there. Hold on."

I went to the search box and typed in Gregg Wakeman and hit enter. I waited for it to dig through its files and then the window popped up with three Gregg Wakemans. I ruled out two because it said they were in other states. The one I liked didn't say where he was from but he wasn't from elsewhere. I clicked on the name and it brought up the profile page. I read it to Lynn, "Well, his screen name is @Arachnid, how appropriate. I would think Stacey could figure out that the guy stalking her and killing people with spiders would be called arachnid. I can't get in his timeline since he's not following me and he's not online I'm sure. Try that on her and let me know."

She said she would and hung up. I was watching the screen of tweets in my timeline, nothing exciting, there never seemed to be lately. I heard the front door open, the tinkle sounded almost like a warning for some reason. I listened for Lacey to ask the question, "May we help you?" The voice from a man said, "Yes, I need a private investigator, I hear this Jim Richards is good."

"Oh, he's the best; you came to the right place." She picked up her desk phone and hit the intercom button and announced that I had someone to see me. I smiled at her professionalism and said to send him in. I didn't feel like going out to greet him, he could come to me, but I did stand for him as he came to the door. I welcomed him, "Come on in and have a seat. I'm Jim Richards." I held my hand out and he came over and took it. His hand felt clammy, I didn't want to wipe my hand and offend him, but I would when I sat. He did sit and I sat, wiping my hand on my pants from under the desk.

"Now what can I do for you?" I asked.

"Well, you can die and go to hell," he said calmly.

"Well, I'm sure to get there one day, but I'm not ready right now." I said wondering what this was about.

"Yeah, well I think you need to go now," he said as he pulled out a gun from his jacket pocket.

I was having flashbacks to all the killers who came to me after a crime to kill me for screwing up their law-breaking. I just sat staring at him then it came to me, "Gregg Wakeman."

"Yes I am, and you and your friends were warned to keep your noses out of my business. But you just couldn't listen, could you."

He was waving the gun around as he talked. I knew I couldn't get to my gun fast enough before he could pull his trigger. I was wishing Buck was here, or Lacey calling the cops, but they might not get here in time, they might just end up carrying me out in a body bag.

"I am not happy about you taking me away from my love. She needs me and I don't even know where she is right now."

"She's in police custody at Metro. She says she doesn't know who you are."

"She knows! She loves me but she is weak, and needs loving, which I want to give her but she has been busy fighting off those other men, these card players, they wouldn't stop bugging her and asking for her to meet them. But I took care of a couple of them."

"Did you know the first man you killed was her husband, Harvey Trent?"

He was silent for a moment taking that in, "She never said she was married. I think you are lying to me."

"Gregg, her real name is Stacey Trent, not LadyLucky, think about it. She never even met him because she didn't want to spoil her fun online if he knew. So you killed him because she talked to him pretending she wasn't who she really was."

He was thinking now, probably trying to remember if Stacey ever did meet with Harvey. I was stalling hoping something would happen.

He jumped up, "You're trying to confuse me, I know I'll find her and we will go off together and be happy." He was scaring me now, his eyes were wild, he was definitely unbalanced. He raised his gun now pointing it directly at me. I had been shot once before when I was in New York, it hurt. Not something I wanted to go through again. He was shaking and now yelling, "You're going to die now! Say good bye to your life!"

I looked down not wanting to see the flash of the gun and the bullet hit me, as I heard the blast. But I didn't feel anything, I looked up and he was gone. I stood and he was on the ground, I looked to the door and saw Lacey with a gun in hand, looking stunned. I went to her taking the weapon, "Lacey, where did you get a gun?"

"It's Penny's, she dropped it off, she didn't want to take it shopping with her. It was in my drawer and I heard what he was saying to you. I'm sorry." She was starting to tear up and I put my arms around her and said she did good. I heard a noise from behind me and looked to see Wakeman holding his gun up. I pushed Lacey into the hallway and turned sideways as he shot, he missed but I didn't. He fell back and went still. I went to him taking his gun and checking his pulse, there was none. It was over.

Lynn was ecstatic now that Wakeman was

found. She was telling Lacey she did good and telling me how lucky I was to have a quick thinking helper. I smiled at Lacey and she asked if she could go sit down, she wasn't feeling well; I told her to go sit. A few minutes later Mac came flying in and rushed to Lacey, they embraced.

Trapper came in and asked what was going on, did he miss something? I said I'd explain later, as they were taking Wakeman's body out in the black bag I thought would be for me. Penny was holding the door open for the ME's men pulling the gurney out. She came up to me and said, "I can't leave you alone for a minute can I?"

I grabbed her, giving her a big smoojie on the lips and thanked her for leaving the gun here, she gave me a blank look, I said, "I'll explain later."

Lynn said, "Stacey did finally remember Arachnid, she said he was nuts and tried to avoid him but he would bug her all too often. Stacey is no longer a suspect, so I guess she will collect her two million dollar insurance pay out. This is just so wrong but what can I do? Oh and she wanted to see Reverend Ben again, they deserve each other. He'll drain her money dry." She looked to Deacon and said they needed to go write up their reports, "Damn I hate paperwork."

We were all in our backyard having a barbecue about two hours later, I closed up the office and everyone was there. After we ate I held up my beer can and made a toast.

"Thanks to all my friends, thanks to all of you for being in my life. The world is now good."

THE END

For every ending there's a new beginning!

PREVIEW OF THE NEXT BOOK

"Vegas Vigilante Murders"

Chapter 1

The house on the far eastern edge of Las Vegas was dark this morning. The only light on was in the hallway outside the bedrooms on the second floor, just outside the open door to Jessica's room. She was an adorable nine year old child, who was just now being beaten by her father, Leo Meyer. Her whimpering and cries only made it worse, as her father was even more enraged by her sobs, so he would beat her harder.

"Shut up!" he screamed as she tried to bite her lip to silence the sobs coming from her bruised throat where moments earlier he near strangled her. "Shut the hell up or so help me I'll make you wish you were dead!"

"Maybe she isn't the one who should be dead," came a soft voice from behind Leo. He paused in his tirade on the girl and turned quickly to see a dark figure silhouetted in the doorway. The light from the hall shone brightly behind the man, his face darkened by the lack of light in the room. Leo reached over to turn on the small lamp resting on the child's bed stand, illuminating the stranger.

The person was dressed all in black clothing; black combat boots, black cargo pants and a black vest that made him look like he was part of a SWAT team. The man's face was hidden by a black mask reminding Leo of an executioner from medieval days.

"Who the hell are you?" Leo slurred from the over indulgence of alcohol he had consumed all morning. "Get the hell out of here, this is personal."

The mystery man stepped backward into the hall and said softly, "Make me leave."

Leo stood the best he could and staggered towards the figure, more enraged than when he beat the girl. "I show you who will make you leave," he spit out the words.

The figure turned from the door and was gone; Leo ran out and saw him standing by the stairs.

Black Widow Murders

Leo charged the man, but when he got to him the dark figure grabbed Leo and with a viscous swing, threw Leo down the stairs. Leo rolled and bumped downward until he came to a stop on the floor, his head twisted in an unnatural direction.

The man came down the stairs and checked Leo's pulse, there was none. Seconds later, the dark figure had vanished from the house.

The Las Vegas Metro 911 dispatcher answered the call and heard a small sobbing voice asking, "Please help me, I think my daddy is dead."

~~*~~

The sun hadn't even risen yet as my darling Penny was having fits about what to wear for her talk show today. She was having three big name male hunks on her show promoting their movie filmed in Vegas. I sat on the edge of the bed as she flitted around the room pulling clothes from the closet over to what was Willy's chair. Willy, our ever faithful toy Yorkie was still on the chair trying to finish his sleep, and didn't seem to be bothered by the ton of clothing piled on him.

I checked to see that he didn't suffocate and turned to my wife and said, "Why don't you just go on the show naked. I'm sure they would love that." My statement was followed by a shoe being thrown at my head, as I retreated to the kitchen. I was trying to make some toast when Willy came flying in. I wasn't sure if he was alerted by my presence in the kitchen or chased out by Penny.

I was sitting at the snack bar munching my toast as Willy munched on his kibble, when Penny came out wearing a short tight black dress, with a string of pearls and long dangling earrings. Around her waist was a wide gold belt and she had matching gold high heels, spiked.

"Are you going out clubbing or hoping to entice one of your stars today?" I asked.

She stuck her tongue out and said, "I have to project an image of glamour for my viewers." She bent down to get a pan from the bottom drawer in the stove riding her dress up and exposing her lace underwear.

"The only thing you're going to project is those great black panties you're wearing," I smirked.

She quickly stood realizing what she had done, looked to me for a moment and went back to the bedroom, whacking my arm as she passed.

She settled for a white silk blouse and a slightly longer skirt that wouldn't expose her to the lecherous panderings of her guests. I smiled at her as she stuck her tongue out again. She poured water in the pan and set the burner to heat the liquid. She then poured the oatmeal in as the water rolled and steamed.

237

Black Widow Murders

"So what are you going to do today?" she asked me.

"I have a small case to find out if a wife is gambling the family savings away. Her husband can't quite seem to be able to follow her, since she only goes out while he works, or so he thinks. I have to sit out front of the house and follow her to see if she is playing games of chance with their life savings."

"Sounds like fun, don't get distracted by all the lovely women in the casinos."

"I keep my focus on the case, not the bevy of beauty found around the high rollers. Actually most of the women in the casinos are ordinary wives or plain Jane types. The really good looking ones are in the private rooms for the big spenders, the whales."

"Well, remember the beauty you're married to. I don't want to ever find you chasing a skirt without a case behind it."

"Yes dear. Oh, Buck picked up a new account for his guards yesterday. They will be guarding all the Gas-N-Go stations around Vegas. It should be very lucrative for the firm."

"How do you guys split up the money from all your ventures?"

"All income goes into one account and then we get a salary. It's all for bookkeeping and taxes, but we are investing in a bit in property speculating on expansion of the casinos."

"You'll lose your shirts."

"Thanks for that nod of approval. Shouldn't you be going?"

She looked at the clock, wolfed down the rest of her oatmeal, grabbed her purse and briefcase, kissed my nose and then headed out. I heard the garage door open and her car drove out the drive, setting off the driveway alarm. I went over and reset the thing then returned to my toast.

I had dressed and was getting Willy ready for Lacey to pick him up and take him to our office. I had to go directly to the client's house to tail his wife, so I wasn't going into the office right away. About ten minutes later the drive alarm went off, it was Lacey. I reset the alarm again and then set the thing for twenty minutes to allow me time to leave.

The door bell rang and I had Willy in his purse, his head sticking out of the opening watching the door for Lacey. I opened the door and Willy yipped at Lacey and she yipped back. I know she's a little childlike sometimes and I really believe she can communicate with Willy.

Black Widow Murders

"Good morning Lacey, how are you today?"

"I'm great, Mac got home around six this morning from his guarding the car dealership and we had breakfast together. He said Buck may put him on the gas station detail, which would be nice, it's a day job so we can see each other more often," she bubbled.

"That's great, nothing like passing each other going to your respective jobs."

"Yep, we now get about two hours together evenings and mornings, not much time to do anything other than fool around." She blushed after she said that.

"I understand, sex is a healthy part of a relationship," I smiled.

"Yes, but Mac doesn't like to rush, so our times together are spent fooling around and not getting much else accomplished." She blushed even redder.

"Okay, go before you start looking like a tomato." I laughed.

She thanked me and took Willy in his purse and went off. I gathered up my camera case and a few other things I would need, then went to the door just as my cell phone rang, it was Lynn. Usually when she called me early in the morning it was police business that she wanted to ask me for advice. Although she and Deacon were talking about getting married lately, so I wondered if it could be about that.

"Hello Dick Tracy, how are you this morning and what murder do you have for me to solve?" I said.

"You have a son, so you may know more about children then I do, how do you get a kid to talk when she's frightened out of her skull?"

"Okay, start at the beginning."

"We got a call this morning to 911; a child said her father was dead. When the first responders got there they found him at the bottom of the stairs, dead, and the little girl was too frightened to talk. I would call child protective services, but I don't like those people. I have no experience with children and since you act like a child most the time, I thought you might help. Besides you're the grandfather type, so she might relax around you."

"Thanks for the grandfather comment, I'll remember you in my will. I have a follow the wife case but I can put it off one more day. Where are you?"

"In my office, we brought her here and I think it frightened her even more."

I thought a moment, and then said, "I have to

swing by the office for something and I'll be in shortly." I hung up after she said she'd wait. I thought I may need a weapon to relax the child; I was going to pick up Willy.

**

Continued in the book...

~~*~~

Jim Richards Family of Readers

Thanks to the following people who are now part of the Jim Richards Family of Readers. They have read a book or more and enjoyed them. They all volunteered to be included in the list. If you are a fan of the books, send me your full name and you will be included in future books. Send your name to murdernovels@bobmoats.com to be added here and on the website. (updated 04-02-14)

* Achim Feifel * Al Norris * Alex Wheatley * Alexandra Delporte-Wilkinson * Amy Tapia * Andrea Bryan * Anne Shepherd * Arianda Sugar * Arlene Markowski * Ashley Augustus * Audra Hall * Barbara Hughes * Barbara Sammons * Barbara Schuler * Barbara Zirger * Beth Donohue Plenskofski * Betsy Childress * Beth Gibson * Bill Sandy * Bill Tornquist * Billie-jo Collie * Boni J Rychener * Carl Bishopric * Carla Lewis * Carole Henderson * Carolyn

Bob Moats

Conroy * Carolyn Riddle-Linington * Cassy Bailey * Chad Hudson * Charlotte L Duran * Cheryl L. Everett * Cindy Ackley Nunn * Cindy Valstad * Connie Bancroft * Corinne Kay O'Daniel * Dana Robbins Chuchran * Dana Wichita * Danielle Monique * Darren Heald * Dave Travers * David Wilkinson * DeAnn Jannereth * Deanna Miller * Deb Breuker Balbo * Debbie Carter * Debbie White * Deborah Fartuch * Deborah Gauze * Deborah Sullivan * Dee King * Denise Freeman * Diana Carver * Dixie Beck * Donna Gould * Donna Thompson * Donny Minter * Doris Kight * Eddie Moore * Eric Walters * Felicia Annette Bradfield * Francine Menor * Gail Chesney * Georgiann Minster * George Conner * Greg Colucci * Hayley Rankin * Harold Garcia * Heidi Arnold * Irma Ranee Coy * Jacqueline Moss * Jan Kimball * Janice Schneider * Janice Spoor * Jennifer Redmond * Jessica Keown-Belous * Jim Beck * Jo Boguslaw * Jo Turner * Joanne Marie Turner * John Peiffer * John Wisbiski * Joseph Wauro * Joyce Stacy * Joyce Trifiletti * Judy Franklin * Judy Travers * Judy Padgett * Julie Heath * Junnahvee Benson * Karen Dahl * Karen Grams * Karen Higham * Karen Kaiser * Karen Meinburg Richwine * Karen Kirkman Parker * Karin Hawkins * Karin Vasvari * Kathleen Donohue Roesing * Kathleen Riddle-Wolfe * Kathy Hinds Moore * Kathy Jones * Kathy Mitchell * Katie Benzler * Kay Burns * Kelly Garcia * Ken Boggs * Keota Rodriguez * Kiera Mccarthy * Kim Estes * Kitty Stolle * Kristie Sciler * Kirsty Stanton * LaLonnie Scallen * Larry Morris * Leann Parr * Lenora Scales * Leslie Marie Jackson * Linda Forester * Linda Ingle Cox * Linda Kennerö * Linda Magill * Lisa Bower * Liz Gibson * Lorraine Wiman * Loretta Alexander * Lynda Bowles * Lynette Lawrance * LuAnn Louttit * Manny Rothman * Marcia Gibson DeWitt * Marie Calder * Marlene Bryan * MaryLouise Kramp * Mary Lynn Gross * Megan Atkins * Meghan Hyden * Melody Cannavan * Michael Carruthers * Michael Dinkens * Michael Vannoy * Michelle Burns-

243

Black Widow Murders

Mitchell * Michelle Pilcher * Micki Potter * Mike Moats * Mimi Baur * Myrna Hecht * Nadine Sutton * Nancy Ellen Sayre * Natalie Quine * Neena Martin * O'Della Wilson * Pat Pollington * Pat Rohn * Patricia Jarmon * Patricia C Trezza * Patrick Barry * Paul Lawrance * Peggy Davis * Phyllis Bassett * Raylene Matheny * Rebecca Collins Besner * Renee Brumley * Reta Hanna * Reta Moats * Roberta Navarro-Harder * Sally Berneathy * Sally Hubler * Sarah Santos * Satka Nikc * Sharon E. Edwards * Sharon Mangini * Sharon McMillon * Sheena Rawl * Sherry Amstutz * Shirley Alvarez * Shirley Davies * Shirley Williams * Stacie Rowe * Stephanie Conner * Steve Cullen * Susan Haughton * Susan Hesse Adams * Susan Salomon * Suzan K Chase * Taisha Cullum * Tamara Moore * Tammy Castleberry * Tammy Lynn Wood * Ted Murphy * Terri Atkins * Terri Creech * Terry Raab * Tonia Rachael Riggs-Williams * Travis Fleury-Lopez * Twyla Gawlas * Val Brooks * Walt Munsel * Yvonne Isakson *

Thank you to all these wonderful people.

Thank you for purchasing this book. I hope you enjoy it as much as I enjoyed writing it for my faithful readers. Please feel free to email me to tell me what you thought about my stories. I love hearing from the readers. I can be reached at murdernovels@bobmoats.com thanks again!